Books By Daniel Landes

Hang the Innocent (2022)

Bowl Off! (2023)

The Amish Cookie Bandit (2024)

The Amish Cookie Bandit

By Daniel Landes

ACKNOWLEDGEMENTS

To my wife, Martha Kemm Landes, for her endless help editing, formatting, and the overall production of this book.

I would also like to thank Dr. Stephen Hollender, an Ohio German professor, for his advice regarding my use of the German language in this book.

PREFACE

The Amish, a branch of the Swiss Brethren, descended from the Anabaptists of sixteenth-century Europe, many of whom settled in Pennsylvania, Ohio, and Indiana. Traditional members are known for speaking and writing a unique language called Pennsylvania Deitsch. Its origins are Germanic, coming from Europe and more specifically from several regions in Switzerland, Germany, and Russia. Most Amish Americans are trilingual. They speak Pennsylvania Dutch at home, Old Amish German in their religious services, and English in public. They know English quite well because it is taught in Amish schools until students graduate from the eighth grade, a compulsory education requirement.

To avoid confusion, my Amish characters speak mostly English with German accents. However, I have added a few touches of Pennsylvania Dutch and German to create linguistical authenticity.

"Be life long or short, its completeness
depends on what it is lived for."
Amish Proverb

Chapter 1

Lancaster County, 1971

It's a warm and humid fall day in Dutch Country. An Amish settlement, bordered by the Susquehanna River, is eerily silent as a pale-feathered barn owl with long wings and a short, squarish tail drops from the cloudless sky. It lands on a rooster-shaped weather vane on the roof of Moses Hochstetler's red barn and flutters its wings. The bird turns its head and looks down on an "Old Order" Amish farm centered by an ivory-colored house that's surrounded by a recently painted white picket fence. Next to the home is a well-tended garden with a *Wizard of Oz* scarecrow and row after row of tomato plants, sunflowers, and green-leafed vegetables.

The owl flies off, soaring above golden wheat and ready-to-be-picked corn fields. Every half mile a neighboring barn and silo is bulging with fresh-cut hay and bags of grain.

On the community's only tar-paved road, two single-seat carriages approach each other. They are both being pulled by look-alike black standard-bred horses with blinders. A full-bearded Amish man, dressed in a straight-cut black coat, doesn't slow as he doffs his broad-brimmed hat at almost fourteen-year-old Noah Hochstetler and his eleven-year-old brother, Eli, headed the other direction.

Sporting straw hats and long-sleeved flannel shirts too warm for the day, the brothers spit dust and rub their eyes. Noah, a handsome boy with long blonde hair and matching eyebrows, loosens the reins to the horse, while his red-headed brother studies the cornfields on his right. Further down the road, red silos and red barns dot the landscape as the Hochstetler brothers pass six bearded married men and four clean-shaven single men picking corn at a brisk pace.

The Amish farmers are dressed identically in black broadfall trousers, solid white shirts with one gray suspender, and wide-brimmed straw hats. The men give the boys a courtesy wave and they wave back.

Two younger farmers, their sleeves rolled up, stop what they're doing and remove their hats. Their hair is bowl-cut in the front and shoulder-length in the back. An older man frowns and the youngsters go back to work tossing corn into the bed of a draft horse-drawn wagon.

Minutes later, the Hochstetler boys drive past another white house, where they see a forty-year-old Amish woman in a solid black dress with a white cape that covers her bodice. At her side is her twelve-year-old daughter, holding two wicker baskets. Donning a starched white organdy cap, the girl drops the baskets and starts hanging up men's blue work shirts, gray socks, and black pants. She arranges them on the clothesline according to size. For some reason, she holds up her mother's undergarment and snickers. When she sees the Hochstetler brothers riding away, she waves the bloomers like a white flag. Her mother notices and slaps her on her bottom. The girl smirks and hides the unmentionable behind her back.

A mile down the road, **the** wheat fields glisten as Noah steers the horse-drawn buggy off the main thoroughfare and onto a dirt road bordered by a pine log fence.

Noah snaps the reins to the horse and the animal breaks into a run. The older brother laughs as Eli grips the leather seat and hangs on tightly. Having had his fun, Noah yanks the reins, and the carriage slides to a stop. The horse snorts and paws the ground.

Noah enjoyed scaring his younger brother because Eli was easily frightened. With a heavy Pennsylvania Dutch accent blended with English, he says, "Du piss dein pants, bruder?"

Eli smirks. "Nae. Dat var lustig, but Vader will see our horse's sweat and take the strap to us."

Noah's brother was right. Their father would probably find out he had raced the horse and take the leather strap to them. His motto was "Spare the rod and spoil the child." For some reason, Noah was different from the other boys his age. The temptation to do something wild would always bubble up inside him and he couldn't help but act on it. For a brief moment, he would forget his father was an Amish bishop and that his brother couldn't keep his mouth shut. He tried to adhere to his father's rules, but when he was alone with Eli, the desire to do the devil's work was sometimes too hard to resist. Noah wipes his brow and says, "We will wait for him to kuhl before we go home."

Eli sighs, "Noah, warun du und dein freund Malachi sprechen so much of der Englisch?"

"We swear in German don't we?" But Eli was right, he and his friend Malachi stopped speaking Pennsylvania Dutch to each other and almost everyone else six months ago, except for their parents. Like everyone in the community, he was trilingual. He spoke Pennsylvania Dutch at home, read and sang German in church, and wrote and recited English in school. He didn't know why he was so fond of English. Maybe it was because he liked the way it sounded when he read it out loud in school. His teacher, Miss Thompson, even bragged to the rest of the class about how good he was at pronouncing difficult English words like pneumonia, mischievous, and synonymous.

Behind them, a carriage approaches with two fifteen-year-old Amish boys, Amos King and Daniel Miller. Amos rolls his rig up to the Hochstetler's buggy and gives Noah a fake smile. "Dummkopfs. Rass du to Mill Creek Bridge."

Noah's first thought was to tell Amos to go to hell, but he tried not to swear unless it was necessary, especially around Eli. His father insisted there be no cussing at home, but he always felt there was a time and place for it, especially if he kept it inside his head. The way he figured, if he didn't take the Lord's name in vain, what was the harm in it? But instead of cursing at Amos, Noah scrunches his face and snarls, "Ich don't think so schwein face."

Seated close to Amos, Daniel Miller spits out a mouth full of sunflower seed shells and points at the Hochstetler brothers. He grunts, "Chicken scheisse."

Noah didn't like being called a coward and wanted to tell Daniel his mother and sisters looked like pigs. But instead, he slaps leather to his five-year-old quarter horse and the animal gallops off. Eli flies back in his seat, grabs Noah's arm, and hangs on for dear life.

The race is on as the Hochstetler boys' buggy opens a healthy lead over Amos and Daniel's rig. Scared to death, Eli starts to sing in German the traditional hymn *How Great Thou Art:* "Oh herr, mei Gott... wenn ich mich in ehrfurchtgebietendem staunen wundere... Betrachten sie alle... Die welten, die deine hände gemacht haben... Ich sehe die sterne...."

The Hochstetler carriage wheels rattle violently and the kerosene lamp hanging from the roof swings wildly from side to side as Amos and Daniel try to close the gap.

Noah sees the Mill Creek Bridge ahead as fifty-year-old pig farmer Beiler "The Butcher" Bontrager pulls his buggy to a stop on a side road. Belier watches closely as Noah and Eli speed past, followed by Amos and Daniel.

A hundred yards from the bridge, the Hochstetler horse sees

a rabbit crossing the road and swerves to miss it. The rig starts to tip over, but somehow Noah keeps it upright as it slides off the road. When the left rear wheel hits the drainage ditch and a huge rock, the impact destroys three wooden spokes and bends the iron rim. Noah lowers his head, grits his teeth, pounds his knee, and screams, "Verdammt noch mal!"

The Hochstetlers boys hop out of their buggy and assess the damage as Amos and Daniel ride past staring at the rig's broken wheel. They give Noah and Eli the finger and Amos yells, "Cow dung!"

Noah unfastens the horse from the broken-wheeled carriage as Beiler Bontrager arrives and checks the damage. He leans over and grumbles, "Gott's plan ist for du to wok." The butcher rolls away smiling and shaking his head.

The boys are silent as they lead their horse down the road. The weather changes as the clouds darken and the wind picks up. A farmer passes them in a corn-filled wagon pulled by a young horse and tilts his hat.

When they arrive home, they see their forty-year-old father, Moses Hochstetler, standing in front of the house smoking a corncob pipe. Moses, who almost always speaks Pennsylvania Dutch, stands six feet tall, walks with a slight limp, and seldom smiles. He is wearing a pale long-sleeved blue shirt with one suspender, a black vest, black trousers, and high-top leather boots. When he sees the boys approaching, he empties his pipe and removes his wide-brimmed straw hat.

Behind Moses is the family home, a clapboard-sided white dwelling that's been recently painted. West of it is a red barn and a matching grain silo.

Moses wipes the sweat from his brow and glares at his sons. "Where ist mei kutsche?"

Eli looks at the ground trying to avoid looking at Moses's steel-gray eyes. Noah shifts to English while his father continues to speak Pennsylvania Dutch. "Two miles down der road... for sure a broken wheel."

"Why ist it brechen?"

"Ich drove the rig into der hole."

"Why in der hole?"

"Der horse took us there."

"Why would er take du there?"

"He saw a rabbit … der hase."

Noah could hear a voice in his head whispering, *Okay, no lies so far, but it's just a matter of time before he tells one.*

Eli shifts his body, looks up, and says, "Vader, wir war racing der buggies with Amos King und Daniel Miller."

Moses lowers his voice. "Racing?"

"Ja. Zu der Mule Creek Brücke."

Noah wanted to say *Why can't you keep your mouth shut, Eli?... Du pissant.* Avoiding eye contact with his brother and father, Noah looks at the barn, where he sees Beiler Bontrager's buggy.

Like a witness for the prosecution, Beiler strolls out of the barn and joins the Hochstetlers. The pig farmer sighs and says, "Ich can kommen on Tuesday and slaughter them if du want."

Eli looks at the butcher as if the man is talking about slaughtering him and his brother. Beiler notices and cackles. "No reason für der angst. Du two Runts are safe. Du doesn't have enough fleisch on dein bones for das pfund of bacon."

Moses returns to his conversation with his oldest son. "Why does it take so lange for der truth to kommen out of dein mouth, unlike dein bruder?"

Noah kicks the heel of his boot into the dirt and speaks in English. "I was paving my way to a full explanation... elüuterung."

"Du will sprechen our language… just like dein family!

"Du speak with sprinkles of Englisch. Why can't I?"

"Ich am der Vader. Du will gehorchen… obey." Noah doesn't say anything else so Moses continues, "Der truth is du went on die joy ride with dein bruder."

"Es war fun."

Moses spouts scripture in English. "Fun? 'When childish people go down the wrong path, they will die. And when foolish people are satisfied with the way they live, they will be destroyed.'"

Noah doesn't back down. "The Gott I know isn't going to destroy me for accidentally damaging a buggy wheel."

"Backpfeifengesicht! Du will honor dein Vader and dein Mutter, das dein days may be lang…."

Noah holds his hands at his side like a traitor at his court marshal and says, "Was ist mei punishment… mei bestrafung?"

Moses narrows his eyes. "After du komplett dein chores, du will remove der mist from der scheune and put it in der garten. After das du will scrub der scheune floors… and nae diner for du or dein bruder."

With a huge aggrieved sigh, Noah composes himself and turns away. He didn't mind scrubbing the floors in the barn, but making them go without dinner was cruel. His father would never let one of his animals go hungry. Of course, why should he expect anything else from the man? After all, he wasn't a pig whose value depended on his weight. He was only his son.

Before he finishes his thought, Eli asks, "Will I be helfen Noah clean der scheune, Vader?"

"Nae, after dein licking, du will help dein schwesters waschen der dishes and der clothes."

Noah sees the fear in his little brother's eyes as the boy's pants darken. He hated that Eli was about to get the strap for going along with his choice to race a couple of idiots who were probably at home right now laughing.

Eli whispers to his father. "Will Noah get der licking zu?"

"Dein bruder ist past der lickings Sie have all been for naught."

Noah's anger wells up as he walks away muttering, 'I'm tired of all your shit-talk old man."

Moses raises his voice. "Was dat du sagen?"
Not turning back, Noah finally tells a lie. "Wondering what der meal ist ich will be missing tonight."

As Noah and Eli walk away, Moses recites a passage from Proverbs in English again. "Pride goeth before destruction; a haughty spirit before a fall."

The frustrated father shakes his head and turns to Beiler. "Mei sohn ist as stubborn as a mule in der shade."

Beiler grins. "Ich wonder where der boy gets das? Kommen. Let's get dein buggy."

The sun sets as Noah leaves the barn with a wheelbarrow filled with chicken and pig manure. When he reaches the garden, he empties the contents and spreads it like chocolate frosting on a cake. From behind the house, he hears his brother Eli scream every time his father slaps him with a leather strap.

Noah returns to the barn, drops to his knees, removes a large sponge from a metal bucket, and scrubs the floor. He didn't mind shoveling cow and pig manure, but he hated the sound of his little brother crying out in pain. He would have offered to take Eli's place, but he knew his father would have nothing to do with it.

He hated to admit it, but he enjoyed the pungent odor of the barn and the blend of animal smells that flavored it. Maybe that was a good thing because he heard Beiler say pig mist was the smell of money. Noah finishes his work, tosses the sponge, and spits on the floor. He walks out of the barn with the bucket and tosses the liquid fertilizer into the pig pen.

That evening, seated around a large handmade dining room table Moses built himself, the Hochstetler family eats dinner. Moses is at the head and his thirty-eight-year-old wife, Ruth, is on his right. She is a tight-lipped woman, whose hair is tied in a neat bun on the top of her head. Her face reveals that her beauty has been diminished by hard work and little joy. On her side of the table sit twelve-year-old Sarah, eight-year-old Mary, and Anna, age four. Next to Moses are Noah and Eli's empty chairs, seven-year-old Samuel, and six-year-old Jacob. Moses bows his head. The family follows suit and they pray silently.

While the family eats a meal of roast pork, garden peas and carrots, and homemade bread, on the other side of the house Eli lies on his bed whimpering. Across from him on a larger bed, Noah snickers. "See what der truth gets du... a good thrashing and no dinner."

Eli rolls over and faces his brother. "Dieses dein fault."

Noah reaches under his pillow, removes two chocolate chip cookies, tosses one to his brother, and keeps one for himself. Eli gobbles it down. Next, Noah produces two small bags of potato chips. He throws one to his brother, opens a bag for himself, and stuffs a handful of chips in his mouth.

Eli licks his lips, opens his bag, and nibbles on a chip like he's a gopher trying to make it last. "Noah, why du all the time angry?"

Noah grins. "Kummerspeck. It's mei grief bacon."

They finish eating and Noah turns down the kerosene lamp.

In the dark Eli whispers, "Are du not going to tell dein bruder gute nocht?"

"Gute nocht, truth-teller."

"Gute nocht… liar."

When Noah closes his eyes, he realizes his brother is right. He is a liar, but not like the wooden boy, Pinocchio, he read about in school… who lied about everything. He was more of an exaggerator like his best friend Malachi Yost, who claimed he had sex with three girls at some secret party he had in his cousin's barn. Lately, Malachi had been bragging about getting drunk on his father's whiskey. The way he figured it, there were lies of deception and lies of exaggeration. Lies of deception caused more harm than lies of exaggeration. Maybe he had groped a girl or two or even sipped the devil's brew, but that's about it. That's the thing about being a good liar, nobody knows for sure if you're telling the truth or making things up. Eli on the other hand was honest to a fault. He wouldn't tell a fib if his life depended on it.

Unable to sleep, Noah rubs his upper lip where he feels a little hair starting to grow. Eli begins to snore, so he reaches under his pillow and removes a transistor radio. He tunes in a station, lowers the volume, holds it to his ear, and starts listening to a rock and roll song. He whispers to himself, "Thou shalt not have any fun… Moses one, verse thirteen."

The next morning Noah and Eli stand in the barn's hayloft pitching straw into the pig corral below. Noah opens the loft door wider and smiles at his brother. "Go on! Don't be a coward."

Eli never wanted his brother to think he was afraid to do anything, but he wasn't a daredevil like Noah; he didn't like to take chances. Besides, whenever his brother talked him into doing something he didn't want to do, he ended up getting a licking. Eli steps back. "Warum du jump aus der barn roofs?"

"I'm an einhorn… a unicorn… one of a kind. Now jump."

"Gonna be late for schule."

"Chicken scheisse." Eli doesn't move, so Noah shrugs, leaps out of the barn, and yells, "Geronimo!" Noah waves his arms mid-air like a baby bird and lands feet first in the pig corral. Pigs scurry as he looks up and signals Eli to jump.

Eli looks down. "Warum du scream Geronimo?"

"Army paratroopers yell it when they jump out of airplanes." Noah waves at his brother. "Hurry up! You're walking on mei cake."

Eli hesitates, closes his eyes, and mutters, "Geronimo." He drops from the loft, lands awkwardly in the straw, and spits. He stands up, grabs his leg, and limps off.

Noah, still sitting in the hay, laughs. "Du all right?"

Eli whines, "Nae, I'm crippled for sure."

Chapter 2

On a cool fall morning, smoke bellows from the brick chimney of a white clapboard one-room schoolhouse with cement steps and a large cast iron bell next to the front door. The Amish men of the community built the school five years earlier when the state of Pennsylvania threatened to have the Amish children bussed to Strasburg if the settlement didn't construct an official schoolhouse and require their children to attend school through the eighth grade or until they turned fourteen.

Not far from the building are two small outhouses. One of the privy doors opens and six-year-old Lars Gruber exits, fits his suspender, and runs for the schoolhouse door.

Inside the crowded building, twenty-five students, ages six to fourteen, study quietly in the crowded room as Lars slides into his handcrafted wooden desk and opens his history book.

In the row next to him sits Noah, who is eyeing his twenty-two-year-old school teacher, Mavis Thompson. As the first-year instructor writes the names of three states and their corresponding capital cities on the chalkboard, he studies her shapely bottom and long legs. Two girls behind him notice him staring at her and start to giggle. Unlike the white-capped Amish girls dressed in long-sleeved grey blouses and full-length black dresses, the attractive auburn-haired teacher is wearing a below-the-knee plaid skirt, a white blouse, and a yellow cardigan draped around her shoulders.

Noah took a special interest in Miss Thompson six months earlier when she replaced Fritz Bauer, an ill-tempered middle-aged man who decided to raise cattle and sheep rather than look after his neighbors' children.

Even though Noah knew Miss Thompson was an outsider and older than him, he couldn't help but lust after her. He was the best student in the class, but he spent most of his time fantasizing about what it might be like to have Miss Thompson as his first girlfriend.

Noah wakes from his dream when Miss Thompson pivots away from the chalkboard and says, "Here are three more capital cities and the states where they are located. I would like you to put them to memory."

Mavis points and everyone, including Noah, studies the board. She waits a few seconds and erases the city names. She smiles and then points to each of the state names. "Okay, everyone… Texas?"

Students answer in unison, "Austin."

She continues. "California?"

"Sacramento."

"Nevada?"

"Carson City."

"Good. Put your books away now. It's time for recess. No lollygagging today. You have one minute to return to your desks after I ring the bell. We have penmanship to work on today."

The students rush out the door giggling as Noah approaches Mavis, sitting behind her desk and staring at her left hand. She looks up. "Why, Noah? You startled me. Aren't you going outside? It's a beautiful day."

"May I talk with du a moment, Miss Thompson?"

"So formal. Of course. What's on your mind?"

"I'm a good student."

"You're my best scholar. I think you know that, Noah."

"Mei birthday is next week."

"Yes, fourteen. You are going to finish the school year, right?"

"Only if mei Vader will allow it. But the Old Order Amish way is for me to farm full time."

"I am well aware. And I know you didn't start first grade until you were seven, like many other children in this school. And for those who started earlier, they repeat the eighth grade, even though they don't need to.

"That's because…"

Mavis cuts Noah off and raises her eyebrows. "I know. Parents don't want their children to attend high school in Strasburg, so they have them put off graduating until they turn fourteen. Will you be happy working on the farm?

"Nae, ich want to attend high school and maybe even college. Will du help me with that? Maybe du could change my vader's mind."

"I'm an outsider… Englisch. When I took this job, I promised the school board I wouldn't encourage any of my students to seek an education beyond the eighth grade. Your father is a board member, so I'm afraid I would need his support if I were to talk to you about furthering your education."

"So, if he gave du his permission, you'd tell me to keep going? Right?"

Mavis laughs. "You're my best mathematician, writer, and a terrific reader. Your achievement tests are the highest in the county. If I had your father's support, I'd love to recommend you go to high school in Strasburg, but you didn't hear that from me. What would you want to do after high school?"

"Join the Army."

"Really? You don't have to graduate from high school to do that?"

"But I want to be an officer, so I'd have to attend college."

"There's a crazy war going on in Vietnam right now. Young

men dying over there every day. You know that, right?"

Noah takes a moment. He hadn't thought that much about the dangers of war, but being a soldier seemed like a much better choice than working with a man who treated him like a slave. The only thing he had in common with his father was his last name. They never had any fun together, because all he wanted was to do was check his crops and care for his animals.

Instead of complaining to his teacher about his home life, Noah says, "I wanna see the world, not the back of some mule. Do you have any books I can borrow that tell what it's like to be a soldier?"

"I am only allowed to provide you with reading material approved by the school board. I'm pretty sure books about military life and war are not on their list."

Noah frowns. "Ordnung."

"Ordnung?"

"Old Amish rules and outdated ways of doing things."

"Yes, the Amish, in general, are not so fond of the contemporary world of art, music, and theater... not to mention the military."

"Ich don't see what's wrong with reading about the real world... even if I never get to see it."

"Oh, Noah, I can't..."

"Please. I won't tell anyone I got the books from you. I'll say I found them or some stranger gave them to me."

Mavis hesitates, grabs a key, and opens the cabinet behind her desk. She removes two books and hands them to Noah. "I read these in high school. Both novels have soldiers who are very young. Anyone finds out I gave these to you, it could cost me my job."

Noah reads the book covers aloud: "*All Quiet on the Western*

Front"... The Red Badge of Courage. Thanks. I'll bring them back as soon as I finish reading them."

Mavis removes a cloth bag from her desk and hands it to him. "Don't let anyone see them." Mavis watches as Noah hurries to his desk and puts the bag inside it. She smiles. "Now go outside. You still have a few more minutes."

Noah looks at two small paintings of owls on his teacher's desk. "One more question. Why do you like owls so much?"

Mavis smiles. "Owls are symbols of wealth, prosperity, wisdom, good luck, and fortune."

Noah grins. "Good to know." He hustles out the door and sees twenty-plus children playing in front of the school. He walks to the back of the building, where he finds thirteen-year-old Malachi Yost smoking and eating an apple. Malachi hands his friend a cigarette and tosses him a small box of matches. Noah strikes a match and lights the cigarette.

Malachi, who has pockets of intelligence, speaks English almost as well as Noah. He's the same height, has a prominent chin, and is forty pounds heavier because he's always eating. Malachi flutters his eyes at Noah and hums *When the Saints Go Marching In.*

As the boys puff away, Malachi asks, "What were du doing in there with Miss Thompson... jumping her bones?"

"Du have a wild imagination. Dein mind is always in the pigsty." Noah coughs, puts his cigarette out, pulls a cookie out of his pocket, and starts to eat it.

Malachi tosses his apple core and stomps out his cigarette. "Give me one of those." Noah removes a second cookie from his pocket and tosses it to him. He grins and says, "Ich see the way du study her ass."

"Don't start any trouble. Ich only have a week left of school."

"Why only der week?"

"Told du. I'm turning fourteen and mei vader is making me quit school."

"Must've been drunk when du told me."

"Never seen du drunk in mei life."

Malachi ignores what Noah just said. "Lucky. Got two months 'til I'm done."

"Du wanna quit. I don't want to dig in the dirt and raise pigs der rest of mei life. I like school."

"What du like ist Mavis Thompson."

"She's Englisch. I have no chance."

"So, du are hot for her?"

"She is easy on der eyes."

"Ja, she makes me feel funny in mei trousers too."

Noah grimaces. "Let's change the subject."

Malachi hums *When the Saints Go Marching In* again. He stuffs a handful of sunflower seeds in his mouth and starts spitting the shells. "Gute news? I'm starting a gang."

"What kind of a gang?"

Malachi flutters his eyes. "Friends doing crazy scheisse."

"Define scheisse?"

"Stealing, burning things, chasing girls, drinking, and smoking some of that funny weed they're selling ."

"Who's gonna be in this so-called gang of yours?"

"Everyone and no one. Calling ourselves der Whiskey Boys."

"Have you ever tasted whiskey?"

"Bottles more than du can count."

"You all the time lying. I never know what to believe."

"Gonna feckin join or not?"

"I'll hold off for now."

"A lamb afraid to be a lion." Malachi hums his favorite hymn again as Miss Thompson steps out of the schoolhouse and rings the bell. The students groan and run for the door.

Noah and Eli lay in their beds with the lights out. Eli sees a flashlight come on and looks over at his brother. Noah sits up, pulls a blanket over his head, and starts to read *All Quiet on the Western Front*.

"Was du tun?"

"Reading."

"Der girly Zeitschrift?"

Noah lowers the blanket. "Ja… *Big Jugs*."

"Let mich sehen."

"Nae."

"Ich saw Mutter's jugs."

"Liar."

"Ask ihr if du want. Sie wur taking der bath. Nicht sehen any other naughty parts though."

"Gehen zu sleep."

"Sie screamed like die stuck sow."

"How about I come over there and thump du on der melon?"

"Nae, I'm schlafen now." Eli closes his eyes and Noah grins and starts to read again.

Chapter 3

Inside the Hochstetler barn, Beiler "the Butcher" Bontrager, wearing a blood-soaked white apron, finishes dressing out the second of two large sows hanging from a chain attached to the barn's center beam. He lays down his knife and admires his work.

Noah and his father wipe their bloody hands on their aprons and Moses points at two nearby gut buckets filled with pig intestines. His son picks them up and heads for the door.

From the time he was a little boy, Noah had mixed feelings about slaughtering living things. He knew Amish farmers believed God created certain animals for human consumption, but he had reached a point in his life when he wasn't sure he agreed with that anymore. He didn't dare share how he felt with his father, because he knew he'd quote some Old Testament scripture verse at him proving him wrong.

What he did know was if he did end up being a farmer, he wouldn't have any pigs, chickens, or cows. He would only grow corn and wheat... and wouldn't be some religious zealot telling everyone what they should or shouldn't believe. He'd take his time and decide for himself if there was a God and whether or not life had a purpose It was getting harder and harder to keep his mouth shut, but what choice did he have? He had no money. And where would he go? He needed a place to live.

When Noah returns to the barn, he sees his father using a large bladed saw to cut the hind quarter off one of the pigs. Beiler removes his apron and hands it to Noah as his father puts the meat in a burlap bag. Moses slaps the butcher on the back, hands him the sack, and removes his apron. "Dunke schön, Herr Bontrager."

Beiler looks over at Noah. "Könnte use dein son's help at mei place on der Samstags. Pay would be fair... Zansig dollars. Gut praxis."

Moses doesn't wait for his son to answer. "Er will be there next Samstag."

Noah raises up. "Saturday ist mei only free day."

Moses turns to Noah, hands him both aprons and says, "Du need money of dein own."

As Beiler leaves the barn, he turns to Noah and says, "Kumme Samstag morning at sieben. Mei schwein are early risers."

Beiler leaves and Moses points at the blood on the floor. Waschen sie die blood off der floor, bevor sie kommen in der haus." Irritated, Noah removes his apron and tosses all three of them on the floor. The Amish pig farmer growls, "Bringen sie diese zu dein Mutter for der wäsche."

As Noah bends over to pick up the aprons, he clears his throat and says, "Vader, ich wish to go to der gymnasium in Strasburg."

Moses tilts his head back. "Nae. Du are done with der schule. Die Bibel says, 'Do not love der world or der things in der world. If anyone loves der world, der love of der Father ist not in him.'"

"But ich love schule."

"Nae, kommen dein birthday, du will quit die schule, work on der farm, get baptized, and finden der frau to start der familie mit."

Noah knew arguing with his father would do no good, but he couldn't help himself. "Vader, ich wish du respect du, but ich don't want to live dein life."

"Der farm ist Gott's place for der familie. Moses takes a step and turns back and stares at Noah's face. "And remove der vanity von dein lip before der diner."

Moses starts to leave again as Noah turns angry. "I hate being

Amish! And I'm never getting baptized!"

"Nae diner for du." Moses stomps off, leaving Noah with tears of anger.

While the Hochstetler family eats their evening meal, Eli looks at Noah's empty chair. When he is sure no one is looking, he lowers his head and whispers a prayer. "Gott, please be with mei bruder. Make his head not so strong."

Now in their shared bedroom, Eli watches as Noah reads *The Red Badge of Courage*. Eli finally breaks the silence and says, "Why du not Sprechen?"

"I'm angry and want to hold on to it. I'm a German like you."

"Ich ate dein share of der brode, fried chicken, and mashed potatoes."

"Goody two shoes."

"Why du make fun of me?"

"Who says it's fun?"

"Saved du some cookies." Eli tosses his brother three cookies… one at a time.

Noah grunts, "Danke, doofus."

Eli grins. "Bitte, doofus."

Sitting at a picnic table next to the barn, Moses and his sons, Noah, Eli, Samuel, and Jacob are whittling. They are each armed with a carving knife and a block of basswood. The younger boys, Samuel and Jacob, struggle as they try to shape something recognizable out of their pieces of wood, so Noah and Eli try to help them.

Moses, who is busily crafting a walking stick, looks up and gives his four sons a rare smile. The boys don't notice as they concentrate on their projects.

It's early morning and Noah is slumped over on the steps of the schoolhouse, his hat on his lap. Next to him is the book bag Miss Thompson gave him. The schoolhouse door swings open and Mavis walks out, but Noah doesn't move. She sits next to him and waits. When he doesn't speak, she says, "What are you doing here so early? School doesn't start for another hour."

He hands her the book bag. "Here are your books."

"Finished already? What did you think?"

"The soldiers, Fleming and Baumer, are cowards."

"War will do that to you. Those young men discovered that fighting a battle wasn't as glamorous as they thought it might be."

"Now, you're preaching at me."

"I'm sorry. I wanted you to see that being a soldier might not be what you think it is, especially if people are shooting at you."

Noah stands to his feet and backs away. "I'm going now."

"Not waiting for school to start?"

"Today's my birthday."

"Happy birthday, Noah. I take it your father won't let you finish the school year."

"Be working from sun up to sundown, except for the Sabbath."

"Did you tell him you wanted to go to high school?

"He doesn't care what I want. All he does is hammer me with scripture. Says I'm a disobedient son who is in love with the world. Old is best. New is of the devil."

"Maybe something will change and you'll discover a road that will take you where you want to go."

"I'm Amish. The only road out of this place is for horses and buggies. I'm stuck here for the rest of my life."

Mavis stands up. "I was speaking metaphorically. Stay put. I'll be right back." She enters the schoolhouse with the bookbag, while

Noah sits back on the steps.

She returns with an official-looking piece of paper and a full bookbag. She hands the document to him and he looks at it carefully.

"What is this?"

"Your graduation certificate."

"I didn't graduate."

"You more than graduated."

Noah peeks inside the bag and Mavis pats him on the shoulder. "More books for you to read."

Noah tries to hand the bag back. "I can't take these."

"No, it's okay. Bring them back when you want some more."

There's a moment of silence as Noah turns serious. "Have you ever kissed a man?

Mavis blushes. "That's rather personal, don't you think?"

"How about bundling? Have you ever bundled with anyone before?"

Mavis thinks for a moment. "Bundling, like cuddling or spooning? Yes, I've done that before."

"When I turn sixteen, I will be eligible for rumspringa."

Mavis smiles. "Rumspringa... exploring the outside world and dating?" Noah stares, points his finger at Mavis, and grins.

"What? You're not suggesting you'd like to date me when you turn sixteen, are you?

"That would be all right with me."

Mavis laughs. "I'm twenty-three years old, nine years older than you... an outsider. Englisch. I'm sure you'll find yourself a wonderful Amish girl someday."

"I like older women."

"Noah, I'm engaged to be married." He studies her left hand and she smiles. "My fiancée and I are saving up for an engagement ring. I am leaving at the end of the school year."

Noah tightens his lips. "Perhaps you will have a falling off."

She smiles. "A falling off? Don't think so. He's a special man…. one of a kind."

Noah reaches into his pocket and pulls out a wooden figurine. He hands it to Mavis. She looks at it closely. "An owl. Did you make this?"

"T.H. White said, 'Owls are the most courteous, single-hearted, and faithful creatures living.' I am single-hearted for you Miss Thompson."

"Noah, that's so sweet. I'm sorry."

Noah stands. "I'd better go." He takes a step and turns back. "Maybe I should kiss you goodbye?"

Mavis leans back. "Don't think that would be a good idea."

"I guess I won't see you again."

"Come back for a visit any time you want... until the school year ends. I will give you more books to read."

"Nae, it would be too painful to see you."

Noah hands the bag of books to her, fits his hat, and walks off. Mavis sighs and goes back into the schoolhouse.

Chapter 4

FOUR YEARS LATER

Under the sweltering summer sun, Noah, almost eighteen, hoes the dirt around a row of corn in a large field. Exhausted, he removes his wide-brimmed straw hat and wipes his brow. He's taller, has more muscle weight, and his hair touches his shoulders.

An hour later, he repairs the barbed wire fence lining a cattle pasture. He finishes digging a hole with a post-hole digger, drops in a wooden post, covers the opening with dirt, and attaches the wire. When he looks up, he sees his sister, Sarah, coming his way with a bucket of water and a bag of cookies. She has a lasting smile and is a younger version of his mother. Noah sits, she joins him and they start to eat the cookies. She ladles water into a tin cup, hands it to him, and he gulps it down.

Noah loved his brothers and sister but sometimes they were too nice. Except for Eli, they all had the same personality and no sense of destiny. And like the other Amish children in the community, they always did what they were told to do. They were perpetually happy, never sassed their parents, and even seemed to like going to Sunday church and other religious gatherings.

Lately, Eli had developed a rebellious attitude but was better at hiding it from his parents and teachers than Noah. Perhaps that would change, like it had for him. Nevertheless, Eli was still his favorite sibling. Maybe it was because they shared a room and a lot of secrets or possibly because he knew his brother idolized him.

Over the last four years, every week was pretty much the same for Noah except for Saturdays. He enjoyed hiking the two miles to Beiler Bontrager's farm, where he fed his pigs, cleaned manure out of the pens, and sometimes helped the farmer butcher a sow or two. He felt more important at Beiler's place like he was his equal and not a son who was expected to do more than his share of the work around the farm. Noah had saved most of the money Beiler had paid him, six hundred dollars hidden in his room.

Noah arrives at Beiler's place at exactly seven a.m. as usual. The old farmer's homestead is a little more run-down than the other Amish farms in the community. His house and barn need painting and the only time Beiler takes a bath is when he gets caught in a rain storm. He has been letting things slide, but no one complains, because Beiler's wife died two years earlier of liver cancer. After her death, the farmer lost interest in almost everything, except his pigs. He did however maintain his side hustle helping his neighbors butcher their livestock.

With a handkerchief covering his face, Noah guides one of Beiler's pigs into a narrow wooden chute, where the butcher brands the animal on its right flank. The three-hundred-pound sow squeals and kicks its feet as Noah hops out of the way. Beiler laughs and Noah guides another pig into the chute.

Finished for the day, the farmer and his hired man sit in front of the barn smoking pipes. Noah points at the setting sun and Beiler hands him ten dollars. He stuffs it in his pocket and jogs off.

After Noah arrives home, he walks to the well and pumps cold water into a bucket. He removes his shirt and cringes as he scrubs the pig odor from his skin with a bar of homemade lye soap. Two Amish teen girls walk past the house, spot the bare-chested Noah, and giggle as they scurry off. Moses, watching him from the barn door, stares until Noah sees him and puts on his shirt.

The Hochstetlers are eating their evening meal, seated in their usual places. The children look older now, especially Eli, fifteen, who has gained ten pounds and grown two inches taller.

Moses leans back in his chair and belches and Noah and Eli follow suit. Sarah smiles, covers her mouth with a dinner napkin, and belches into it. The younger children laugh and belch as well.

Ruth Hochstetler smiles and stands up from the table as the children prepare to take their dishes to the kitchen. "Stoppen! War haben der cake." She leaves the dining room but quickly returns with a large birthday cake with eighteen candles. She places it in front of Noah, strikes a match, and lights a candle. Then she uses the burning candle to light the smaller ones. "Gute gubbotta dawg, mei sohn. Mai Gott's blessings shine on du from heaven above."

Noah blows out the candles and smiles. "Danke, Mutter." He turns to look at his father, but Moses looks away.

Ruth cuts the cake and hands everyone a piece. She signals Eli, and he removes a present he's been hiding under the table. He softly places it in front of his brother.

The other children yell in unison. "Open! Open!"
Noah carefully unwraps his present. Inside, he finds a large black leather-bound Bible. He looks at it and says, "A Bibel."

Ruth leans over. "Nicht just any Bibel. Dein GroßVader Stolfuz's Bibel. Er read it every tag."

Noah stares at it for a moment. "Danke, but wouldn't du rather save das für someone else who…"

His mother interrupts him. "Mei Vader's Bibel goes to der oldest sohn. Right, Moses?"

Moses snorts. Wir should wait for his baptism. Bring es mir."

"Embarrassed, Noah hands his mother the Bible and she

walks it over to Moses. He opens it and reads in English: "Children, obey your parents in the Lord: for this is right. Honor thy father and mother; which is the first commandment with promise; that it may be well with thee, and thou mayest live long on the earth."

Noah furrows his eyebrows. "Don't forget the next verse. 'And fathers provoke not your children to wrath, but bring them up in the nurture and admonition of the Lord.'"

The children look at their father and back at their brother. Ruth changes the subject. "Do not forget it is dein Vader's turn to preach in der morgen, so wir haben to leave early for der Hoffmann-Haus." Ruth smiles and the children attack their cake.

That evening on the rooftop of the Hochstetler barn, Noah shines a flashlight as he stands next to the rooster-shaped weather vane lit by a full moon. Next to him eating a ham sandwich and spitting tobacco juice is Malachi, who has gained thirty pounds in the last four years. Noah shakes his head. "How do you do that… chew tobacco and eat at der same time?"

Malachi, whose deep brown eyes sometimes out-talk his tongue, spits a wad out of his mouth and grins. "Practice, mei boy, practice." Still best friends, Noah and Malachi have been so busy farming, that they have hardly had a chance to hang out with each other. A year earlier, Malachi had quit smoking and eating sunflower seeds, but he had taken up chewing tobacco. Noah asked him why and he said chewing was better than smoking cigarettes and spitting seeds because it was a two-for-one. He could get his nicotine fix and spit at the same time.

In the pig corral looking up at the flashlight is Eli. Not far from him, six pigs huddle in the corner grunting and squealing. Malachi moves to the edge of the barn, flutters his eyes, and steps back. "Du ist crazy. Ich nicht doing das." Noah grins and tosses his hat to test the wind. He shines his flashlight on it and watches as the hat floats to the ground.

Malachi turns to leave. "See du on der ground, doofus."

Noah grits his teeth. "Chicken."

"Rather be a live chicken than a dead duck."

Malachi hums *When the Saints Go Marching In* as he descends the ladder and walks over to the pigpen. As he sides up to Eli, he signals Noah to jump and stuffs his mouth full of more chewing tobacco. He turns to Eli and says, "He'd better hurry up. Ich got three women on mei list of things to do."

Eli grins. "Noah says you lie a lot."

"Here's what I know. The truth is not the truth if no one believes it and a lie is not a lie if everyone believes it."

"Ich don't know what that means."

Malachi chuckles. "Here's Gott's truth. Dein brother's about to kill himself."

Eli shakes his head. "Er does das all der time."

On the barn roof, a slight breeze comes up and the weather vane moves. Noah looks down, uses his flashlight, and surveys the large pile of straw next to Malachi and Eli. He checks the weather vane and removes an egg from his pocket. He holds it out, testing the wind, and lets go. It lands at Malachi's feet and the yolk and shell splatter his boots. Malachi spits out a mouthful of chew and yells, "Dummkopf!" Then he watches as his friend aims his arms as if to make a swan dive. Instead, Noah steps forward and free falls, his flashlight flashing. Just before he reaches the ground, he flaps his arms like a featherless turkey and yells, "Geronimo!"

At that moment, a one-year-old pig squeals and runs past Malachi and Eli. They step back just as Noah lands full force on the pig's body, crushing the animal to the ground. The pig grunts once and rolls over dead.

Noah lies on the ground stunned by the fall but manages to sit up. As he looks himself over, Malachi checks out the pig with his friend's flashlight. "He's a goner. Flattened him good. Think du gave him a heart attack."

Noah crawls over and caresses the pig's head like the animal might come back to life. "Vader ist gonna kill me for sure."

Eli panics and runs for the house. Noah yells, "Don't du say a word truth teller!"

Malachi turns to Noah. "Why ya du such crazy-ass schiesse?"

"Overstimulation calms mei nerves."

Malachi looks at the lifeless pig at his feet. "Du sure calmed der swine's nerves."

Noah panics. "Kommen, du need to helfen me."

The eighteen-year-olds struggle as they pull the two-hundred-pound pig into the barn, Malachi says, "Hope dein pa ain't a pig counter."

Sabbath morning, Moses enters his barn and finds a butchered pig hanging from a chain attached to a ceiling beam. As he examines the swine's carcass, his face reddens, and he screams, "Noah!

When Noah enters the barn dressed for Sunday service, he lowers his head when he sees his father staring at the pig carcass. Moses swings around. "Du butcher mei schwein?"

"Er war dead in der pen last nocht."

"Du did not tell me?"

"Ich didn't want to upset du before Sunday service."

"Wie did das schwein die?"

"Ich heard pigs can have heart attacks."

"Er war a jährling." Moses takes a final look at the pig and walks off grumbling. "Du owe a hundert dollar."

A hundred dollars? Noah knew he had made a mistake, but he had butchered the pig and the meat was still good. No sympathy. And why would a father charge his son for the accidental death of a farm animal, especially when the son had never gotten paid for any of the work he had done around the farm? A hundred dollars… five days' work at Beiler Bontrager's farm. He hated his life and started thinking about running off again. But it was the same old story. Where would he go, where would he live, and how would he get there?

It's early Sunday morning and walking down the road in a line in age-descending order are Moses, Noah, Eli, Samuel, and Jacob. Headed for Sunday service, they are wearing their best black coats, hats, and pants. Moses is carrying his large black leather Bible.

Behind them, also in a line, are Ruth and the Hochstetler daughters Sarah, Mary, and Anna. They are wearing black dresses and black high-top Oxford shoes. The girls' black kapps contrast with their mother's white kapp.

The Hoffmann's modest home is filled with forty-plus people in family groups ranging from four to ten members, who are dressed in similar Amish fashion.

Some of the older Gmay parishioners are seated on wooden benches while the Youngie family members are standing and singing 'S Lobg'sang (*The Hymm of Praise*) a cappella and in German: "O Gott Va-ter/ wir lo-ben dich/ Und dei-ne/Gü-te preu-sen;/Dass du une O/Herr gnü-dich-lich,/An uns noun/ hast ve-wei-sen,/Und has uns/Herr su-sam,-men gfürht,/Uns zu er-mah/nen durch dein Wort,/Gid uns Ge-nad su die-sem."

The singing, which is long and drawn out, finally ends and

Moses steps to the front of the congregation. Everyone sits on pine benches as the bishop opens his Bible, raises his chin, and looks at his family seated near the back of the room. Moses lowers his voice and begins. "Praise Gott in der highest."

The congregation responds in unison: "Praise Gott in der highest."

With a stoic voice, Moses announces: "As a reminder, our Sunday service will be held at mei home in zwei weeks. Danke to der Hoffmann family for hosting today's service. And let us not forget to pray for der Troyer family whose barn burned down on Thursday. Wir are making plans for a barn raising soon… and praise be to Gott for another healthy Hershberger child."

Moses nods at John and Edna Hershberger, seated on a bench in the second row next to a non-Amish family of four from Florida dressed in tropical clothing. Edna is holding the Hershberger newborn and sitting between her and her husband are their six-year-old twin daughters. The proud father yells, "Es name ist Daniel… after mei GroßVader! Oh, and diese are our friends from Minnesota visiting us for der week… Gus and Mindy Olsen and their children Curtis and Loretta."

Several people chuckle and begin to talk. Moses smiles and holds up his Bible. Everyone turns silent. "Let us turn to Romans 12:2." He pauses and says, "Ich will read it in der Englisch version in honor of our Englisch-speaking guests. 'Be not conformed to das world: but be ye transformed by der renewing of dein mind, that ye may prove what is der good and acceptable and der perfect will of God.'" Moses scans the room and narrows his eyes on his oldest son as he continues in English. "We are God's chosen people. Some would say we are a peculiar people."

Two young men near the back of the room snicker. Moses glares at them and they lower their heads, so he continues: "But what communion should light have with darkness? With our appointment comes responsibility to God and family. Our principles, which are found in our Ordnung, clarify for us what is considered worldly and sinful. To be worldly is to be lost. Therefore, wir must separate ourselves from the world and dare to be different. Self-denial and obedience to der Word means wir are in full fellowship with God and our family. To disobey His Word or der words of one's earthly father are one and der same. Sin."

Noah grits his teeth and looks away as his father drones on. Trying to ignore the sound of his voice, he closes his eyes and thinks about Mavis Thompson. Eli notices and elbows his brother in the ribs. Noah sits straight up and says, "Owwh! Was?" Ruth points her finger and the boys turn sober.

In the next few days following Sunday service, Moses Hochstetler exalted the virtues of family, the importance of cleanliness, and the requirement of honoring one's father and mother. Noah was relieved when Saturday came, so he could leave the house, even if only to take care of Beiler's pigs.

As Noah walks down the road to Beiler's farm, he sees Malachi and his four Whiskey Boy gang members. The youngest boy has a rope tethered to the neck of a black and white Hampshire pig with the Bontrager brand on its flank.

The other boys laugh and carry on as they watch the thirteen-year-old try to wrangle the pig in the right direction. When they reach Noah, Malachi steps forward and spits out a wad of tobacco. "Where du going barn jumper?"

"Bontrager's place."

"Still a Saturday pig farmer, huh?"

Two boys pinch their nostrils together, while Noah stares at the roped hog. "That's one of Beiler's pigs."

34

"He'll never miss it," Malachi says.

"Ja, he will. Counts them every day."

Malachi grins as he blinks. "Not gonna squeal on us are du?" The younger boys laugh at his joke.

"What you planning to do with it?"

"Having us a royal feast tonight. Gonna put an apple in its mouth and roast him over a fire. You come. I'll even let you eat the apple."

"Vader won't let me out of the house tonight. Tomorrow's der Sabbath."

"It's off Sunday. No services."

"Doesn't matter. Be preaching at us all day like the rapture is at our doorstep."

"He'll let you go to der sing-along tomorrow night won't he?"

"I don't know. Maybe. Never been to one before."

Malachi opens a candy bar and puts all of it in his mouth. "Better come. A good place to check out der ladies."

The other boys snicker as a black Buick approaches carrying a family of tourists. The car slows and a middle-aged man rolls down his window, preparing to take a photo.

Malachi raises up. "Was zur hälle?"

The intruder doesn't respond, so Malachi pulls a pistol from the back of his pants and points it at the driver. The man panics, lowers his camera, looks at his wife and two kids, rolls up his window, and speeds off.

Malachi gives the tourist the finger. "Ficken English!" Two other boys flash their middle fingers as well.

Noah steps forward. "Where'd du get der gun?"

"Mei cousin. Ich can get du one. Twenty dollars."

"Nae. Had to pay mei vader a hundred for the pig I killed."

"Eli tell on du?"

"Nae, not this time."

Malachi puts his gun away. "Sure, du don't wanna be a Whiskey Boy, now?"

"Burned the Troyer barn down, didn't du?"

"It was old. Why? Du need something burned?"

"I'm good. Ich have to go. I'm going to be late."

"See du at der singalong, pig killer."

Noah starts to walk off, but Malachi yells, "Halt!" Noah turns back and Malachi points at the thirteen-year-old boy. "Give him du pig."

Noah says, "What?

"Beiler will take one look at your face and he'll know he's missing a pig. Tell him du found der schwein on der road. That part's true."

The boy removes the rope and Nataniel unfastens his suspender and puts it around the pig's neck. Malachi grins. "One more thing. Das fire was an accident. Wir war shooting off der bottle rockets and one landed on der roof of Troyer's barn. It started to burn, so wir ran off."

"Why du all of a sudden telling der truth and giving things back?"

"Du got me feeling all guilty… schuldig. Ich might wanna be a fancy deacon like dein old man." Malachi grins ear to ear at the thought and hums *When the Saints Go Marching In* as he and his gang walk away.

Noah couldn't picture him as a church leader, but he let it go. When he was eight he had witnessed his father become a deacon. One Sunday service, several men's names were written on slips of paper, put in a black box, and one name was drawn out… Moses Hochstetler. People claimed God had spoken and they prayed and sang a lot of songs. As far as Noah was concerned, it was all a matter of luck. After his rise in the church, his father became even more strict. Although he didn't say it, he started to adhere to the old saying, 'Children should be seen and not heard.' After that, he didn't dare mention he wanted to join the Army because his father's first sermon as a deacon was all about the evils of war.

Later that afternoon at a large waterhole near the Hochstetler farm, Noah and Eli splash each other and play tag. On the shore, next to the water are their folded clothes, straw hats, and boots.

Suddenly, out of the trees walks eighteen-year-old, Rebecca Pearson and a few steps behind her fourteen-year-old Teresa Smith. Rebecca is a large girl with long pigtails. Her cheeks are decorated with red rouge and her eyes are blackened with dark eyeliner, eye shadow, and too much mascara. Teresa is half Rebecca's size, has a freckled face, and is wearing an Amish cap. Despite the heat, she also has on an oversized blue wool sweater.

Noah and Eli don't notice as the visitors park next to their clothes. Fifty feet away, Noah and Eli take turns trying to dunk each other as the girls watch, trying not to giggle.

Finished with their fun, the brothers are headed for dry land when they spot Rebecca and Teresa. Surprised, they step back and squat back down in the water. Noah sputters, "Why du here?"

With a heavy German accent, Rebecca says, "We're der Rettungsschwimmers. We've kommen zu make sure du don't drown."

"Those are our clothes."

"Ja, and sie schtinke like schwien mist. Wir bewachen sie for sie… because we're nice like das."

"They smell bad because ich just finished working with Bontrager's pigs. Why are du guarding them?"

"So, der wind doesn't blow them away."

"It's not windy."

"But it's gonna be. Isn't it, Teresa?"

Teresa blushes but doesn't say a word. Irritated, Noah emerges from the water with his hands covering his private parts and says, "Look if du want. I'm going heim."

The girls scream, jump up, and run for the trees. In the distance, Rebecca yells, "Now du have zu marry mich, Noah Hochstetler!"

It's Sunday evening and the Hochstetler children finish clearing the dinner dishes and head to their bedrooms. Alone at the dining room table, Moses and Ruth remain seated.

Moses lights his pipe, eyes his wife, and begins to think about his oldest son. He couldn't understand why Noah was so stubborn and different from his other children. Did the seed he planted seventeen years earlier fall on unfertile ground… into the proverbial thorns and rocks? Maybe Noah's spirit, like a dormant kernel, would sprout and grow any day now. Maybe God was testing his patience like he had tested Job's.

Ruth stares at her husband's glazed-over eyes and says, "Was ist it, Moses? Du sehen deep in gendanken."

"Du think, our sohn ist a bad seed?"

"Nae. Der buwe ist fine. Jungen take länger to mature than maedels."

"Er has too much hochmut. Er loves der world more than Gott."

"Wir all struggle with der pride, Moses. The difficulty is a miracle in its first stage."

On cue, Noah exits his room dressed in his Sunday best.

Ruth raises up. "Wo du gehen dressed in dein finest?"

"Zu der Sonntag sing along."

Ruth studies her son for a moment and speaks slowly. "Gehen along dann." Noah hurries out the door and Ruth turns to her husband and smiles. "Das ist something."

Moses blows a puff of smoke and looks away.

Chapter 5

It's early Sunday evening as young Amish men and women, ages fourteen to nineteen, file into a large barn, including Amos King and Daniel Miller, the Mill Creek Bridge buggy racers. Last to arrive, Noah stops at the door and thinks about whether to go inside. He wondered why he was there. Sure, he was eligible to date now, but he didn't like to sing and the only female he had ever had feelings for was his teacher, Mavis Thompson.

He hadn't seen Mavis since the day he quit school. He never bothered to ask anyone if she got married, because he knew it would only interfere with the fantasy that he might see her someday and want to hook up.

Noah slaps the side of the barn and quietly makes his entrance. Once inside, he sees a dozen young ladies and ten young men seated at a large table, the girls on one side and the boys on the other. The barn floor is covered with loose straw and alfalfa bales, and the walls are decorated with horse tack, ropes, pitchforks, and shovels. An old broken-down hay wagon sits in the corner with two Eastern Wild Turkeys perched on top of it. Chickens wander around cackling, while two grey draft mules stand in a corner stall half asleep.

As the teens sing in German *Just a Little Talk With Jesus* a capella, Noah walks over to the table, sits next to Malachi, and listens. *"And when you feel a little prayer wheel turnin'… And you will know a little fire is burnin'… You will find a little talk with Jesus makes it right, right, right, right."*

The song ends and the boys jump up and form small groups

a few feet from the table. While they talk, the girls eye the young men and giggle. The girls grow bored and start playing Botching, a favorite clapping game. They pair up, face each other, and slap their hands together while tapping their feet in a rhythmic pattern. They end their game when they slap each other's kneecaps and laugh. Still restless, the braver girls leave the table and mingle with the boys.

In a corner, Noah and Malachi stand together checking out the girls still seated at the table. Noah nudges Malachi. "Das ist lame. Diese girls are as plain as a bar of soap."

"Warte, here kommes mei cousin."

Rebecca Pearson, who has even more makeup on her face than at the swimming hole, skips over before Noah can leave. With a heavy German accent, she says, "Hallo Malachi... Noah."

Malachi gives her a fake grin. "Becca."

"Ich see du bad boys here eyeing der girls. See anyone du like other than me?"

Malachi squirts tobacco in the straw near her feet. "Nah."

She hops back. "Gross." She circles the soiled straw and cozies up to Noah. "Du remember me, dein very own lifeguard? Kann ich get du some lemonade, Noah Hochstetler?"

Noah slowly moves away. "Nae. How du know mei name?"

"Du sat behind me in der school for zwei years. Du war smart and der silent type. Mei folks are gone for der weekend if zu like to kommen zu mei haus. Wir could bundle if you like."

Noah narrows his eyes. "Bundle? We just met."

"Bundling ist a gut way zu get zu know each other. Malachi and ich bundled... didn't wir Malachi?"

"Til ich found out du war mei cousin."

Noah glares at Malachi. "Du didn't know she was dein cousin?"

"No one bothered to tell me."

Rebecca grins. "Second cousins… but Malachi war a gentleman and kept his pants on." She snickers. "Nothing going on down there anyway."

Malachi spouts, "Besserwisser… know it all!"

"Du two are dull." She strides off, sidles up to another boy, and winks at Noah.

Malachi elbows Noah. "Don't get an offer like das every day."

"Ich hate pushy girls."

"Ja, she's schlechdi, but bad girls can be fun if du know what ich mean. Better than force-cuddling dein cat."

"Don't have a cat and don't want none of your scraps. Does she always paint her face like that?"

"Nae. Her folks think she's a saint."

"I'm going heim."

"Es ist early. Stay." Malachi runs over to the table, finds his coat, and removes a transistor radio. He slides back over and finds a rock and roll station. Malachi flutters his eyes and raises his voice. "Hey everyone, time for der hop!"

Noah points. "Ich have a radio just like that."

Malachi turns the volume up and several of the teens gather around him. Not satisfied, he pulls a harmonica from his pocket and plays it to the beat of the music. Everyone laughs and the girls lift their dresses above their knees and spin in circles. In the corner, an older couple does their version of the Twist.

As the music blasts and things get wild, Amos and Daniel hurry out of the barn and return with a wooden keg of homemade Amish beer. While several couples dance in place, Rebecca and a few girls join Noah and Malachi. The remaining younger Amish teens at the table watch nervously as Amos and Daniel pour the beer. Finally, they look at one another and hurry out of the barn.

Malachi and Noah join the dancers. Rebecca notices, moves over, and whispers in Noah's ear. "Du think I'm fett?" He doesn't respond, so Rebecca says, "Mutter says ich have big bones. Du like big bones, Noah?"

Noah ignores her and watches as a Plymouth Rock rooster attempts to mount a German Langshan chicken. The hen tries to escape, but the rooster crows and has his way with her. The mules react to the commotion and bray and kick the stall walls. Rebecca grins at Noah. "Du like to watch chickens do it, don't du?"

Noah steps over to Malachi. "I'm leaving."

Noah hurries out the door and Malachi hands Rebecca his radio. "Give it back tomorrow."

Once outside, Malachi spots his friend and chases after him. When he reaches Noah, he grabs his arm, leans over catching his breath, and says, "Der night's young. Let's whoop it up, go to Strasburg, see a movie."

"Have du met mei Vader?"

"He'll be sound asleep when du get home. Live it up. It's der New Amish way."

"You're not New Amish."

"Not yet, but mei cousin is. He has a phone in his house and even owns a tractor."

Whenever Malachi wanted to do something stupid or break the law, he would claim it was the New Amish way. Noah knew his friend didn't have a religious bone in his body, and he also knew Malachi could talk him into doing just about anything he wanted him to do… kind of like the way he was able to manipulate his brother Eli. The temptation grew inside him like the lust he felt when Malachi offered to loan him a girly magazine that had a naked woman in it who looked like Mavis Thompson. He took it home and looked at it more than he wanted to. Was he about to sin again?

He hadn't been to Strasburg for over a year. Ignoring the voice inside his head, Noah shrugs his shoulders and says, "We are we going to do, borrow it and drive it to Strasburg?"

"Ich have me a car."

"Nae."

"Ja, ich du. Bought it last month. Been hiding it in my cousin's barn."

"Ich know him?"

"If du like apples ya do. Ezra "Apple Orchard" Williams."

"Ich know I'm going to regret das."

"Komme! Was could go wrong with Malachi Hezekiah Yost at dein side?"

As Noah and Malachi walk through Ezra Williams' orchard, a cloud of blossoms fills the air with the scent of rotting apples fermenting on the ground after the fall picking.

The friends sit inside a light blue 1964 Chevy Impala in Ezra Williams' barn. Malachi starts the engine and backs out as chickens run in every direction.

On the outskirts of a small town, they drive past a sign reading "Strasburg, Pennsylvania---Population 2800." Malachi looks at his friend who hasn't spoken in ten minutes. "What's goes on in das head of yours?"

"Mei father's a light sleeper."

"Du think too much."

Noah looks out the front window and says, "Ich think, therefore I am."

"Du make that up?"

"Rene Descartes, French philosopher."

Malachi thinks a moment and says, "Ich yam what ich yam... Popeye der sailor man!"

He laughs at his joke as Noah shakes his head and says, "Ich hate spinach."

Malachi turns serious. "Okay. We'd better speak the King's English when we get to Strasburg if we want to land us some women."

Noah grins. "You lead the way and ich… and I will follow."

Minutes later, Malachi parks his Chevy in front of the Imperial Theater on Strasburg's main street. The multi-colored marquee with flashing red and yellow bulbs reads: "*The Godfather,* starring Marlon Brando and Al Pacino."

The movie starts as the boys enter the dark and nearly empty theater. Malachi is carrying a bucket of popcorn, a large Coke, and a package of Red Vine licorice. They find seats in the third row and plop themselves down. As Malachi gobbles down popcorn, they watch the Francis Ford Coppola film. A violent scene ends and Noah turns and sees two seventeen-year-old girls a few rows behind them who giggle and gawk at the oddly dressed Amish boys.

Noah whispers something in Malachi's ear and they both turn and look at the girls, who giggle even louder. Malachi points to himself and Noah. The blonde and brunette pat the seats next to them and the boys hop up and join the young ladies.

As the girls continue to whisper to each other, their new friends concentrate on the film. The movie ends and they walk out of the theater, sizing each other up. The brunette quickly joins Malachi, while the blonde scoots over to Noah.

Parked on a side road, overlooking the town lights, Malachi is snuggling in the front seat with the brunette, while the blonde and Noah sit in the back seat a few feet apart. The blonde makes the first move as she reaches over, removes Noah's hat, and puts it on her head. "I like your hat and one suspender. Where's the other one?"

"That's all ick have."

The blonde giggles. "Did you just say ick?"

"It's the same as I."

Malachi turns back and holds out a bottle of whiskey. "Looks like du two could use some of der liquid courage."

Noah gently takes the bottle, swallows a mouthful, and offers it to his date. She waves him off. "Nasty boy, not gonna take advantage of me by getting me drunk." She thinks about it for a moment and reaches for the bottle. "Oh, all right. One sip." She takes a large gulp, covers her mouth, and coughs.

From the back seat, Noah and the blonde listen as the brunette giggles and gasps for air right in front of them. "Careful Dumbo, you're flattening my boobies."

Malachi grins, "What's a Dumbo?"

The brunette laughs. "It's an elephant silly." Malachi lowers himself on her again, and squeals like an elephant.

Not sure what to do, Noah makes eye contact with his date again. She reacts by lowering his suspender and pulling him on top of her. As the blonde rubs his chest, she moans and grabs his crotch. He removes her hand, so she sits up. "What? You don't want to?"

"Can we just bundle?"

"Did you say bundle?"

"Ja, snuggle with our clothes on."

"You want to dry hump me?"

Malachi peeks over the front seat and flutters his eyes at Noah. "Live it up. Show her what you got, Tarzan."

The blonde reaches for Noah's crotch again. He recoils and pushes her hand away a little harder this time. She stiffens, adjusts her clothing, opens the door, and exits the car. She immediately heads to the front of the vehicle, taps on the window, and yells at her friend. "Hurry it up! I got me a dud."

Noah watches from the backseat window as the blonde leans butt-first against the front fender and lights a cigarette. Alone in the back seat, Noah listens as Malachi and the brunette moan until Malachi sighs deeply and says, "Oh mei Gott!"

Out of breath, the brunette murmurs, "You got it out in time, right?"

Malachi whispers, "Ja, it war out." He takes a moment, gathers himself, peeks over the front seat at Noah, and says, "Better get these ladies home. Where's your gal?" Noah points to the sulking blonde outside the car.

As the car drives off, Noah and the blonde are squeezed against opposite door windows. In the front, the brunette nibbles on Malachi's ear. All Noah can think about is what could have been. Why didn't he want to have sex with this girl who was busy hating him now? She was pretty, had all the right parts, and was more than willing. The truth was his teacher's face had kept popping into his head, and all he could think about was how he'd rather be in the backseat with Mavis Thompson.

When they reach a middle-class neighborhood, Malachi stops the car on the side of the street and the girls get out. While the blonde walks off in a huff, the brunette blows a kiss at Malachi. He honks his horn, and she hops in the air. She turns back, puts her finger to her lips, and walks away wiggling her butt. On the corner leaning against a light pole, the blonde gives Noah the finger and joins her friend.

As they drive away, Malachi looks in the rearview mirror and says, "Where to now, Romeo?

Noah crawls to the front seat and joins Malachi. "Home. I

won't be eating dinner with my family for a month."

Headed to the main highway, Malachi takes a drink from the almost empty whiskey bottle and hands it to his friend. "Finish it off."

Noah takes a large swallow, coughs, and says, "Mei Gott that tastes awful."

Malachi takes the bottle back. "Don't drink it for der taste, du ringworm." As he turns onto the main highway, he polishes off the last of the whiskey and tosses the bottle out the window. It smashes on the side of the road and they instantly see flashing red lights in the rearview mirror. Malachi panics. "Gott Almighty help us!

Noah wipes off his mouth. "Vader's gonna gut me like a pig."

"Nae. He won't. We're just two idiots being fools."

A police car pulls up behind the Chevy and Malachi parks on the side of the road. Officer, Rupert Irving walks to the driver's side window, taps on it, and Malachi rolls it down. "Driver's license and registration."

Malachi retrieves his license from his wallet and reaches into the glove box, shielding the officer's view. Noah, however, spots his friend's pistol. Malachi shuts the glove box and hands the policeman his license and registration. In perfect English, he says, "Was I speeding, officer?"

"Stopped you for littering. You threw a bottle out of your window."

"Sorry, sir. It won't happen again."

The officer leans forward. "You been drinking?"

Malachi looks at Noah and turns to the officer. "A little bit."

"I'm guessing you drained that whiskey bottle back there."

"There were four of us."

"I count two."

Malachi continues. "Dropped a couple of girls off a few minutes ago."

The officer checks his license. "Girls? Were they underage like you?"

The policeman looks at Noah, who shrugs his shoulders as Malachi thinks quickly and says, "Nae. They were twenty-one, maybe even twenty-two. They bought der whiskey. Right, Noah?"

"For sure... maybe."

"See now. There's another problem. If you were to show me where they live, I'd have to arrest them for contributing to a minor and the two of you for underage consumption."

Malachi panics. "It was dark. I don't think we could find their place again."

The policeman looks in the back seat and says, "Where'd you get the booze, son?"

"Mei vader's liquor cabinet."

The cop backs away and studies the car's exterior as Malachi whispers to Noah in German. "Hope he doesn't look in der trunk. I got two more bottles in there."

The officer returns to the open car window and stares at Malachi. "I know you boys are Amish, but are you New Amish?"

"Why du ask that?"

"You having this car. By the way, I need to look in your trunk." Malachi lowers his shoulders, gets out of the car, and opens the trunk. Rupert finds three more bottles of whiskey and removes them. "Just so you know, I used to be Amish, so I speak German."

Malachi grimaces. "Are we lucky or what?"

Noah finally speaks. "What district du from?"

"Smicksburg."

"And du gave it up… being Amish I mean?"

"My father didn't want me to keep going to school, but I

wanted to be a police officer."

"Ich want to join the Army and be an officer myself."

"Wife told me about a kid who had the same dream. Maybe you know her. She taught in an Amish school district not far from here."

Noah hesitates. "Mavis Thompson?"

"That's her. That's my wife."

"She was my teacher."

Malachi adds, "Mine too."

"Huh, have to tell her I met you fellas."

Noah closes his eyes. "Please don't."

Rupert shrugs. "I should haul both your asses to jail, you know."

Malachi puts his head on the steering wheel. "My life's over for sure."

The policeman takes a moment and slaps the hood of the car. "Tell you what. I'm gonna let you off with a warning. You sober enough to drive home?"

Malachi sits up and smiles. "Ja, sir. Danke. What about mei Vader's other bottles of whiskey?"

"Keeping them as evidence."

"Ich, was planning to put them back before he knew they were gone."

"Noah whispers, "Malachi, let the man have his evidence."

Malachi smirks. "Okay, enjoy the evidence."

Ruppert removes a watch from his pocket and checks the time. Noah recognizes the hand-carved fob attached to it and says, "I like your owl."

"Yeah, my wife gave it to me. Brings me luck. Be safe."

Rupert walks back to his car and the boys wait for the officer to drive off. "What a rush. Zum Mordsackerment!"

Noah points at the glovebox. "Bet you're glad he didn't look in there."

Malachi reaches into the glovebox, grabs his pistol, and hands it to Noah. "Here, du wanted one."

"How much you want for it?"

"Happy birthday. Ich got two more."

Noah looks the gun over carefully and puts it next to him on the seat. When the police officer drives off, he picks it up again and spins the cylinder. "Do I look like a gangster?"

"Ja, a regular Al Capone. Don't play with it, it might go off.."

Malachi vacates the car, walks to the passenger side door, and opens it. Noah looks non-plussed. "What are you doing?"

"As long as we're breaking laws, you're driving home."

"I've never even driven a tractor."

"Then it's time for du to learn."

The boys switch places and Noah puts the car in gear. As the car creeps down the highway twenty miles an hour slower than the posted speed limit, Malachi smiles. "Drive any slower, der grasshoppers are gonna beat us home.

As Noah slowly accelerates, he thinks about Miss Thompson being married to the police officer and what might have been if he had been just a little older and she had been an Amish neighbor girl looking for the man of her dreams. Then his mind shifts back to the trouble he's about to have when he walks through the door of his house with liquor on his breath. He could picture his father standing on the porch, smoking a pipe, and waiting for him.

Chapter 6

It's the middle of the night and a full moon lights the Hochstetler front porch. Large flakes of snow fall as Noah treads softly through the front yard toward his house. He opens the door quietly, and tiptoes inside. When he reaches the living room, he sees his mother in a rocking chair sewing a quilt next to a dimly lit kerosene lamp. Dressed in a long white cotton nightgown, she looks up and presses her lips together as she says softly, "Wo warst du worden, Sohn? Es ist der early morgen."

"After singalong, ich spent time with Malachi… too much time." Noah knew he was going to have to tell a lie at some point, but he hated that it was going to be to his mother.

Ruth studies her son's face. "Das man-child ist a bad influence on du. How of du alkohol hast du consume… Wein, bier, der whisky?"

"Whiskey, but ich hated the taste."

"Gut. Alkohol ist der devil's brew. Perhaps du are sorry for what du did?"

"Sorry for making du worry… and sorry for du having to wait up."

"Enough zu ask Gott for seine forgiveness?"

"Nae, but enough to ask for dein forgiveness."

"Don't be hartnäckig. Komme, join me in prayer to the heavenly Vader." Ruth kneels in front of her chair and Noah slowly kneels next to her.

"What do ich say?"

"Muss nicht sagen anything. In dein mind ask God for der Vergebung."

"And Vader? Do ich have to ask him to forgive me too?"

"Farmers gehen zu bett early. As far as er knows, du sound asleep." Noah bows his head and begins to pray as Moses watches his wife and son from the dark hallway.

Noah massages his head and frowns at his bowl of oatmeal covered with brown sugar while his siblings eat heartily. Moses surveys his family and raps his spoon on the table. "Die madchen, du'll help dein mutter in der kitchen. Jungen, du will stack die hay bales in der barn. Ich will join du und prüfen dein wirken."

The girls promptly clear the table and head to the kitchen, while the boys put on their straw hats and exit the house. Moses leaves the table and stares out the window as his sons head for the barn. He slaps the window sill and walks into Noah and Eli's room. He scans the area and opens the drawers of the boys' dresser. Finding nothing unusual, he checks inside their shared closet, still nothing.

He looks under Noah's bed, finds a red duffel bag, unzips it, and removes the contents. He examines Noah's transistor radio, tosses it to the floor, and kicks it across the room. Then he pulls out a military history book, a pack of cigarettes, a wrapped condom, and a ticket stub with the name Imperial Theatre on it.

Finally, he removes a tattered pornographic magazine. He opens it and the centerfold falls open. He stares at it briefly and shoves everything back in the bag except for the radio.

Moses vacates the house with Noah's duffel bag. When he reaches the barn, he sees his sons building a haystack. From the top, Noah looks down and his face turns pale when he sees his father clutching his red duffel bag. "Eli, Samuel, Jacob... Geh ins der haus! Sensing their father's anger, the boys hurry off as Moses turns to his oldest son. "Noah, komm down from dort."

Noah hops down from the haystack and Moses throws the duffle bag at his son's feet. He looks up at his father. "Du were in mei room?"

Moses grumbles, "Empty der bag. Demo all dein earthly treasures."

"Why? Du already know what's in there."

"Du ins der gang?"

Noah doesn't answer, so Moses walks inside the barn and returns with a five-gallon can of gas.

A small fire blazes outside the barn as Noah empties the contents of his duffel bag into the fire pit. He watches everything burn and then looks at his son. "Our familie will shun du until der Sunday meeting at our haus. There du will admit dein indiscretions to der entire body. Only after du acknowledge dein transgressions will du be allowed back into our fellowship. After dein confession, we'll make plans for dein baptism. Das ist mei order of obedience."

"Always second saying the Bibel to me. Rules and commandments. Because of you, I want nothing to do with religion."

"Blasphemisch. Du will das der richtige ding… und sprechen der Deutsch."

Noah stiffens and continues in English. "Nae… no! I will speak English… and the right thing for me is to do what makes me happy." He grabs his duffel bag, dusts it off, and heads for the house.

Later that evening, Noah lies in bed in his daily clothes waiting for Eli to fall asleep. His mind is filled with doubt as he considers his situation. Should he ask his father for forgiveness, get baptized, and become a farmer? In his heart, he knew the answer. He wasn't cut out to work in the fields and raise pigs. He wanted to see the world. Maybe, like the prodigal son, he would sew his wild oats, spend the money he had saved, and end up on some stranger's farm sleeping in a pile of pig manure. Then he would come to his senses, return home, and ask his loving father for forgiveness. The only problem was his father wasn't loving and he wanted to join the Army.

When his brother snores, he climbs out of bed and reaches for his shoes. The door slowly opens, so he crawls back under the covers and closes his eyes. His mother enters the room and walks softly over to his bed. She spreads the quilt she just finished making across the foot of his bed and says a silent prayer. Then she places a document, a small card, and a paper bag on it. She steps over to Noah, gently kisses him on the forehead, and leaves the room.

As Eli sleeps, Noah shines his flashlight on the beautiful multi-colored quilt and a bagful of cookies. He notices the documents, picks them up, and sees that they are his birth certificate and social security card. He lays them aside and begins to pack some of his belongings into his duffel bag, including clothes, two books hidden under Eli's bed that Miss Thompson gave him on his last day of school, and his transistor radio.

Next, he walks to the dresser, scoots it forward, and reaches behind it. He removes the pistol Malachi gave him, a stack of money, and a small wooden unicorn he carved a few days earlier. He tiptoes over, carefully puts a miniature horse he carved under Eli's pillow, and puts everything else in his duffle bag.

Before he exits the room, he takes the quilt from his bed and puts it over his shoulder. When he reaches the door, he pauses, steps back, and kisses Eli on the cheek. "Auf widersehen, kliener bruder." Eli starts to stir, so he leaves the room quickly.

He walks away from the house and through the front gate. He hears the front door open and turns back. He quickly ducks down behind the white picket fence and watches his father walk onto the porch smoking a pipe.

As he stares at Moses through an opening in the fence, Noah removes the 38-caliber pistol from his pocket. He aims it at him through an opening as his father looks up at the moon. Embarrassed by what he was thinking about doing, he lowers the gun and puts it away.

After Moses empties his pipe and walks back into the house, Noah stands up and tosses his duffel bag over one shoulder and the quilt over the other. As he walks away, it starts to snow again, so he covers his head with the quilt.

The sun is peaking over the horizon and it's snowing harder as Noah and Malachi walk down a rutted road leading to Ezra "Apple Orchard" Williams' farm. Malachi is carrying his friend's duffel bag and humming *When the Saints Go Marching In*. Noah has his mother's quilt wrapped around his upper torso. "Thanks for this. Owe you big time."

"Just lucky I'm an early riser."

"Sorry, I didn't have anyone else to turn to."

"We friends or nicht? Ich wanted to run away when ich eligible for der rumspringa, but look at du, you're doing it."

"It feels more like a prison break. This uncle of yours, why do you call him Apple Orchard Williams?"

Malachi rolls his eyes. Noah finally understands and grins. "Ahh, because he grows apples."

"There du go, dummkopf. Something else before ich sell du mei car." Noah waits and Malachi whispers, "Join der Whiskey Boys."

"Why? I'm leaving."

"Ich wanna tell der other fellas you're one of us."

"What do I have to do?"

"Nothing. Du are now an official Whiskey Boy.

The snow has stopped falling as the morning sun glistens through several rows of winter gray apple trees, lighting the exterior of Ezra William's barn. They enter the building and once inside, Malachi opens the front passenger door of his Chevy Impala. He removes several documents from the glovebox and stuffs them inside his winter coat. "Du don't need diese."

Noah surveys the barn. "Nice of dein cousin to let du hide dein car here."

"Nicht das nice. Ich work ten hours a week picking apples…. Okay, how much money du got there, soldier boy?"

Noah unzips his duffel bag, grabs all his money, hands it to Malachi, and his friend counts it.

"Six hundred and twenty. I paid a thousand for this ride."

Noah looks away. "Ich got nothing else. Guess I'll be hitchhiking to Philadelphia."

"Christ on a communion cracker." Malachi takes the twenty-dollar bill and hands him back the rest. He spits a wad of chewing tobacco and grumbles, "Membership dues for being a Whiskey Boy." He tosses Noah his car keys, pauses, and says, "Change of plans. Keep der money and du steal mei car."

"What? Ich can't do that."

"Ja du can. Ich have insurance. If you thief it, they'll pay me what it's worth. Been wanting an old pickup anyway."

"I don't know…."

"Here's der dealio. Destroy it when du get to Philadelphia. Not gonna need it in der Army anyway."

"Du want me to demolish der car?"

"Burn it, drive it in a lake or off a cliff. Don't want anyone bringing it back asking questions. Mei folks don't know ich have a car."

"Guess I can do that."

"Don't forget to remove the license plate before du leave it. And no speeding or running through dumb-ass stop signs or red lights. Du has no license or proof of ownership, so du gotta be careful. Hope du got some ID for or der Army or they might not take du?"

"Birth certificate, social security card my mother gave me."

"Gut. Army will wanna make sure you're who du say du are. You're gonna be a hundred percent English before du know it. Another last thing. Get rid of dein accent as soon as du can. English still don't trust Germans cuz of der two wars."

"Think it's weird me wanting to join the Army?"

"No weirder than du jumping off some damn barn roof."

Noah gets in the car, fires up the engine, and starts to back out of the barn. Malachi panics when Noah almost hits the door frame. He holds up his hand. Noah skids to a stop and rolls down his window. "I've never driven backward before."

Malachi grits his teeth. "Use your mirrors, doofus."

He tries again and manages to back out of the barn. Proud of himself, he waves at Malachi and drives away in his own stolen car.

Chapter 7

Driving a car for the second time in his life, Noah navigates the I-76 freeway on the outskirts of Philadelphia. Cars speed past, horns blaring, as he grips the steering wheel and guides his Chevy Impala ten miles mph under the posted speed limit. His spirit picks up when he sees a sign: "Philadelphia - City of Brotherly Love."

He already missed Eli… and his mother. She had always been good to him. The problem was she was a woman who had been raised to believe God's plan was for her husband to rule the home and that she needed to be submissive to everything he said, just like the other married women in the community. If Noah was to marry, he wanted it to be a woman like Mavis Thompson, someone he could talk to about books, history, or maybe even sex. Someone who was not afraid to speak her mind.

When Noah reaches downtown Philadelphia, he finally finds a parking place but struggles to parallel park his car. People on the street stop and gawk as he tries several times to fit the Chevy in the open space. Finally, a large dump truck leaves, making his challenge easier.

He is walking down the street when he stops and stares at the posters in an Army Recruiting Center Office window. He takes a deep breath, opens the door, and walks inside. There he finds two staff sergeants seated at adjoining desks. The recruiters look at the potential wide-eyed volunteer and grin at his unusual clothing. The older sergeant smiles and says, "What can we do for you, young man?"

Noah removes his hat and steps forward. "Ich… I wish to join the Army."

"Really? You're Amish."

"Not anymore."

The older sergeant winks at the younger one. Then he turns back to Noah. "You seventeen?"

"Turned eighteen… last week."

"Happy birthday. Got any proof of that?" Noah hands him his birth certificate and social security card and the sergeant looks them over. "Good. How about a driver's license?"

"Nae… No. Do I need one?"

"Better get yourself one when you get to Fort Benning if you want to drive a jeep or a tank."

"Fort Benning?"

The younger sergeant enters the conversation. "That's where boot camp is."

"So that's it. I'm in?"

The recruiter continues to talk as he pulls out a form and hands it to Noah. "Not quite. Fill this out. Could have used you earlier. Vietnam's almost over."

Noah takes the form and looks it over. "But I can still join, right?"

The older sergeant grins and says, "We got a busload headed for Georgia in two days. You up for that?"

"I'm ready to go, ja."

The older recruiter snickers. "You pass your physical in the morning and we'll swear you in. Need a place to sleep, we have a voucher for the Spencer Hotel two blocks east of here. The doctor will be here at 0 800 hours. Don't be late." Noah salutes the sergeants, and they wag their heads and mouth the word "no." He shrugs and heads for the door.

Noah drives down Highway 1, south of Philadelphia. When he sees a County Road 7 sign, he slowly exits. A minute later, he pulls off the single-lane road into an open field. He grabs his duffel bag, quilt, and a five-gallon can of gas out of the back seat of the Chevy. He hops out, pulls a screwdriver from his pocket, and removes the car's license plate. He unscrews the gas can cap and pours gas inside and on the car's exterior.

He looks around to see if anyone is looking, strikes a match, and lights the car on fire. As the flames engulf the Impala, he hurries over and removes a hubcap.

As the car burns, he scampers across the road and uses the hubcap to dig a hole next to a large white rock. When the hollow is deep enough, he removes some money and the pistol from the bag. He pats the revolver and puts it back in the bag. Then he drops it back in the hole.

He looks around, tosses the car keys into some nearby trees, turns back, and lays the quilt on top of the bag. He covers everything with dirt, stomps it down, and spins the hubcap like a frisbee into an open field.

Noah jogs back to Highway 1, crosses to the other side, holds out his thumb, and a red van slows to a stop. The bearded driver grins and waves him inside.

Speeding down the highway, the flannel-shirted thirty-year-old cranks up the music and takes a toke from his homemade water pipe. The van fills with smoke and the man offers Noah a hit, but he wags his head and looks away.

The van stops in downtown Philadelphia and Noah jumps out. He waves thanks to the driver, rubs his eyes, and starts looking for the Spencer Hotel.

On a cool Pennsylvania morning, several Amish families in buggies and freight wagons filled with lumber and building supplies arrive at Levi Troyer's farm. The men and their older sons grab their tools, while the women and daughters carry food baskets to large tables and lay out a meal. Several children begin to play games, while others watch and learn from their parents.

Among the workers are Moses, Eli, Beiler Bontrager, Malachi, his father, and two younger brothers. Two Whiskey Boys and their fathers arrive late with a wagon full of oak beams. The boys spot Malachi, wave, and he waves back.

It's noon and the barn builders take a lunch break. They eat heartily as the women and young girls serve them large portions of fried chicken, potato salad, fresh vegetables, and big slices of watermelon.

By the end of the day with the sun starting to set, Levi stands with two older men admiring the framed barn with a partially shingled roof. The tired men load their tools and food into the wagons as Troyer family members wave goodbye. They drive their separate ways, prepared to return the next day to finish their work.

Exhausted from his day at the barn raising, Eli lays on his bed staring at the ceiling. He reaches under his pillow and removes the unicorn carving Noah gave him. He looks it over, tosses it on Noah's bed, and closes his eyes. Eli tries to imagine where his brother might be. Was he living with a new family? Did he have enough to eat? Would he ever see him again? Eli sighs, his eyes flutter, and he buries his face in his pillow.

Just east of Philadelphia, a green Army bus merges onto Interstate 95 and heads south for Fort Benning, Georgia. The rain hits the front windshield so hard that the wipers struggle to keep up.

Inside, the bus driver, an Army lance corporal dressed in military fatigues, stares straight ahead focusing on the road. Behind him, thirty recruits, seventeen to twenty-two, sit quietly thinking about what might be in store for them.

A few minutes pass and some of the recruits begin to talk amongst themselves. Still in Amish clothing and donning his black hat, Noah sits alone eating one of the oatmeal cookies his mother baked for him three days earlier.

Two bearded and long-haired red-neck hippie types, seated across the aisle, look his way and grin. Bill Lawson, tall and long-legged, and Dick Long, much shorter with horned-rimmed glasses, are wearing matching tie-dyed shirts and jean jackets. They snicker as they take a good look at Noah's clothes and his unusual haircut. Bill leans across the aisle and says, "Dude. Who does your hair?"

Dick grins, exposing his gold tooth. "Man, I always thought you Amish didn't ride in motorized vehicles."

Bill curls his lip. "Nah, dickhead. Some of them do. Depends on what tribe they're from."

Noah shifts in his seat. "It's called a settlement."

Dick tries again. "Okay, what settlement are you from?"

"Du really wanna know?"

"Sure. Be seeing a lot of each other. We're from Fort Lauderdale. I'm Dick Long and this is Bill Lawson."

Noah says, "Noah Hochstetler… Swartzentruber."

Bill wrinkles his nose. "Wait. Swartzen… what?"

"Mei home… Swartswentruber. Farming community near Strasburg, Pennsylvania."

Bill grins. "Groovy. I like your accent."

Dick parts his lips, revealing his gold tooth again. "Hey, I heard a good one. What do you call something that goes clip clop, clip clop, bang bang, clip clop, clip clop, bang bang?"

Bill rolls his eyes. "How the hell do we know?"

"An Amish drive-by shooting. Can ya dig it, boatman?"

Bill perks up. "Wait. You just called him boatman?"

Dick snickers. "Noah… ark… duh."

"Your sense of humor is lame, man."

Noah takes a moment. "Funny. Ich got one. Du hear about der hippie that got lost at sea? Bill and Dick don't say anything, so he says, "He was too far out.""

The hippies stare at Noah until Dick says, "Ya think because we have long hair and dress like this, we're hippies?"

When Noah doesn't respond, Bill nudges his friend. "Don't be a dick, Dick."

Dick slaps his knee. "Nah, I'm yanking your chain, Amish. That was a crack-up. Didn't know you people had a sense of humor. You always look so serious."

"Not easy to be funny when you're dressed like das." Dick and Bill point at Noah and laugh.

Dick nods. "I'd dump those clothes and clean up that accent if I were you. I hear the Army looks for anyone unusual to make fun of."

Bill shoves Dick. "Like you're not unusual."

Maybe boot camp was gonna be easier than Noah figured it would be. He'd already made himself a couple of friends. He had read about the endless harassment and the grueling physical challenges, but he knew he was in good shape from all the farm work he had been doing. And he was looking forward to not hearing words from the Bible that would be used to shame him.

As the bus approaches Fort Benning, it stops in front of a small shack. The security guard steps into the bus's headlights. He makes eye contact with the driver and waves him through. Just past the gate, the lance corporal pulls up to the curb in front of three gray buildings and the bus stops again.

The door flies open and Master Sergeant Franklin Hanson, wearing a Smokey the Bear hat and a camo uniform, climbs on board and scans the recruits. "Welcome to Fort Benning! Now get off my fuckin' bus!"

The recruits scramble as they grab their belongings and stumble over each other as they rush for the front door. The forty-five-year-old muscle-bound sergeant holds them back as he leads the way. Outside on the tarmac, they are greeted by Gunnery Sergeant Manny Gonzales, a twenty-eight-year-old Hispanic, who is gripping a military-style flashlight. "Three lines ladies! Do it now!" The recruits stagger around trying to create three lines. Slow to react, Noah ends up in the third line.

Gonzales steps front and center and says, "I am Gunnery Sergeant Manny Gonzales and this is Master Sergeant Franklin Hanson. You will address both of us as Sergeant Instructor. When we give you an order, your only response will be aye, aye, Sergeant Instructor. If we ask you a question, you will answer it in as few words as possible. Do you understand?"

In unison, the recruits shout, "Aye, aye, Sergeant Instructor!"

Sergeant Hanson yells, "Can't hear you! Open your fucking mouths ya damn candy asses! Do you understand me?"

The recruits try again. "Aye, aye, Sergeant Instructor!"

Gonzales screams, "Not loud enough, ladies! Drop and give me twenty push-ups!"

The recruits fall to the ground and start doing push-ups. When they finish, they hop up and stand at attention. The DIs walk down the three lines as Sergeant Gonzales shines his flashlight in the recruits' faces. When they reach the long-haired Floridians, the sergeants look at each other and smile. Sergeant Hanson steps back. "Well, what do we have here? Why aren't you two up in Canada with all the other queers and hippies?"

Bill answers, "We enlisted… Sergeant Instructor."

Hanson turns to Gonzales. "Shit… They enlisted."

They continue down the line until they reach Noah. "Looky here Sergeant Gonzales. We got us another weirdo. You Amish?"

"Not anymore… Sergeant Instructor."

Hanson gets in Noah's face. "What's your name recruit?"

"Noah... Hochstetler."

Gonzales cups his ear. "Hock what?"

"Hochstetler."

Hanson adds, "Another one of those runaways? Where'd ya park your horse and buggy, Amish?"

"I don't have a horse and buggy, Sergeant Instructor."

Hanson shakes his head. "That was a joke. You know what a joke is Amish?"

"Yes, Sergeant Instructor, but it wasn't funny."

Gonzales says, "You're starting to piss me off, recruit. Why do you people dress like you're headed to a funeral?"

"These are the clothes I was given to wear, Sergeant Instructor."

Gonzales continues his interrogation. "Not one of those conscientious objectors are you?"

"No, Sergeant Instructor."

Sergeant Hanson takes over. "You're German, right?"

"Pennsylvania Dutch with German roots."

"You a Nazi?"

"American, Sergeant Instructor."

"Say something in German."

Noah takes a moment and says, "Ich möchte ein Americanischer soldat sein."

"What does it mean, Amish?"

"I want to be an American soldier."

Hanson growls, "Sergeant Instructor!"

Noah adds, "Oh... Unteroffizier-Ausbilder."

"I don't like you Amish."

"Sorry, Sergeant Instructor. I want to be a good soldier."

"We'll see about that. Get rid of that German accent... and take that shit clown hat off your head." Noah removes his hat as Sergeant Hanson turns to the other recruits. "All right everyone, give me twenty more push-ups on account of this German here wanting to be an American soldier."

A few recruits groan as Noah's eyes darken. Everyone drops to the ground and starts doing push-ups again.

The next morning, Noah is sound asleep on the top of a bunk bed when two metal garbage cans rattle down the deck of the 4th platoon barracks. He rolls out of bed and hops to his feet. The sergeants wait for the recruits to fit into their civilian clothes, line them up, and march the forty-plus men out of the room.

The first stop is the camp barbershop, where the men stand like sheep waiting to be sheared by three steel-eyed corporals armed with large electric clippers. When it's Noah's turn, he takes a seat in a chair between Bill and Dick, watching their hair and beards fall to the floor. He smiles at the ex-hippies as they stare into the mirror, checking out their bald heads and clean-shaven faces. Dick rubs his bare head, and says, "Far out."

Minutes later, Noah feels a cool breeze hit his head as he and the other 4th platoon members wait for their military clothing.

Once they have what they need, the sergeants march them back to the barracks where they shed their civilian clothes and put on military fatigues, boots, and soft caps. The sergeants call the men to attention and inspect their new look. When they get to Bill and Dick, Sergeant Gonzales chuckles and says, "Who knew there was so much ugly under all that hair?"

Dressed in Army fatigues, Noah and his comrades march in formation along the parade deck as Hanson and Gonzales yell out a cadence. When they reach the physical training compound, the sergeants scream out orders. The recruits respond by doing pull-ups, sit-ups, and pushups while the sergeants run in place.

It's noon in the mess hall and a hundred men sit quietly eating. Seated next to his new-look friends, Bill and Dick, Noah soaks his bread in white gravy. Bill looks down at his plate. "Kind of good, kind of not so good. What's this shit called anyway?"

Dick grins. "You're kind of close. S.O.S.… shit on a shingle. Get used to it. It's the Army's favorite meal."

Bill pokes Noah in the ribs. "How are you doing, Amish? Our fearless leaders sure like to pick on you."

"Just trying to fit in and do what they ask me to do."

On cue, Sergeant Hanson appears at their table. "On your feet germ boy!"

Noah scoots back from the table and spills his drink on his tray. He grabs a napkin and starts wiping the water up. He thinks better of it, hops up, and stands at attention. Sergeant Hanson says, " Did I see you talking instead of eating, Amish?"

"Both, Sergeant Instructor."

"You being a smartass?"

"Nae, Sergeant Instructor."

"Nae? Don't give me none of that kraut talk."

"Sorry, Sergeant Instructor. I do that when I'm nervous."

"Nervous like them Nazis that killed my uncle when he landed on Normandy Beach? Could've been someone from your Hock family. Mowed him down before he got out of the water."

"Mei… my family has been in this country more than two hundred years."

"So, you say."

Sergeant Hanson grabs the metal tray off the table and gives it to Noah. "It's wet. Hold it out so it can dry."

Noah extends it front and center as the recruits from the other tables try not to laugh. Hanson barks, "Straight out!"

Noah tightens his grip as the sergeant glares and says, "What's wrong, Amish? Too heavy for you?"

"No, Sergeant Instructor."

The sergeant picks up Noah's plate and empty glass and puts them on the tray. Then he grabs a water pitcher and fills the glass until it spills over. "It's still wet. Be back in five. Maybe it'll be dry by then." Nathaniel keeps holding the tray out as most of the men finish eating and start to leave the mess hall.

Sergeant Hanson returns to the almost empty mess hall ten minutes later and finds Noah still standing with the tray stretched out in front of him. Noah's arms quiver as the sergeant tests the dampness of the metal platter with his index finger. "Huh, still wet."

The remaining candidates smirk as they walk past the platoon scapegoat headed back to the barracks. Finally, Noah groans and drops the tray on the floor. The glass and plate shatter as he leans over and throws up his lunch. The sergeant steps back and shakes his head. "Bucket and mop are in the kitchen. When you're done cleaning up your shit here, go to the barracks and scrub the floors… all of them." Sergeant Hanson takes a moment and says, "Hear what I said, Amish?"

Noah murmurs, "Ja, Sergeant Instructor."

"Ja? Son, are you trying to piss me off again?"

"No, Sergeant Instructor." As Noah heads for the kitchen, he wonders why Sergeant Hanson is so determined to give him so much grief. He stopped treating the other recruits like they were scum a week ago. Was it because he was Amish or had German blood? Maybe… or maybe the sergeant doesn't think he has what it takes to be a soldier.

Back in the barracks, Noah sits on his haunches scrubbing the brown tile floor with a sponge, while other recruits polish their boots and write letters home. The metal bucket next to him is similar to the one he used to clean the floor of his father's barn.

A private first-class mail clerk walks up to him and asks, "Noah Hochstetler?"

"That is me."

The private hands Noah an envelope. He opens it and discovers it's a letter from Malachi. He reads it, savoring every word:

"Freund, Noah. How's der Army treating du? Du a ~~Allgemei~~ general yet? Gonna try to write das brief letter in der English for du. Ich bin taking a gamble das you're in der boot camp at Fort Benning at all. If nicht, ich guess ich wrote das letter for nothing. Anyway, thought du might wanna know der ~~Versicherung~~ insurance money came through and ich got mich an old Dodge pickup with lots of power. Only ich got no one to show off to, cuz it's still a secret ich drive. Der Whiskey Boys ain't no more. Der little bastards got themselves baptized and started feeling sinful for stealing and destroying shit, so we ran out of things to do. Guess if ich wanna rob a bank or bomb a building, I'll have to do it mei self. Laugh, laugh.

Miss having du around to tell lies to but there are no lies in this letter. Ain't nothing going on in my life, except I'm seeing my second cousin Becca a lot. Guess if you aim at nothing, you are bound to hit it. Saw dein ~~Bruder~~ brother Eli on Saturday. He asked me if ich knew where du were, but ich didn't give du up. Might wanna drop der poor kid a line sometime, so he don't think you're dead or in prison somewhere. Ich don't know why he's so crazy about du. Mei brothers think I'm an idiot. Got nothing else to say now. Hope du don't get killed in battle or sent to some cold-ass place like Iceland or Antarctica. Guess I'd better close der lid das before der monkey gets out. Freund, Malachi"

Noah folds the letter carefully and puts it in his pocket. It was the first letter anyone had ever written to him. Malachi had turned out to be a better friend than he had ever thought he would be. It made him homesick, especially the part about Eli asking about him. Maybe he will go back someday, dressed in a fancy uniform with all kinds of medals on his chest. But first, he would have to survive boot camp and all the shit the sergeants were throwing his way.

Chapter 8

Members of the fourth platoon, C company, are in equal line formation running down a dirt road chanting the Army song, *I Left My Home*. Two out-of-shape bigger men fall back, so sergeants Gonzales and Hanson bark at them to get back in line.

An hour later, Noah and the other four squad members sit in prone positions firing their M-16s at targets fifty feet away. Sergeant Gonzales walks up behind Noah and pretends not to notice as he hits three bullseyes.

Now on the obstacle course, the recruits crawl through mud-filled pits and under barbwire as the sergeants scream for them to move even faster.

The third squad, Noah in the rear, climbs over an eight-foot wall. They drop down on the other side of the barrier, take a few steps, and roll over a series of four-foot-high log hurdles. Up ahead is the final obstacle, Jericho's Tower. The forty-foot-high structure has a platform at the top. When they reach the tower, they find a large web-like netted rope on the front side of it and five single ropes leading down to the ground on the backside.

Sergeant Hanson holds a stopwatch as the five-man squad climbs the tower in record time. At the top, four men grab the ropes on the other side of the platform and start to descend, while Noah watches.

Instead of using a rope like the other four recruits, he screams "Geronimo!" and leaps off the platform. He lands feet first at the bottom of the tower, just as his comrades hit the ground and release their ropes.

Sergeant Hanson studies his stopwatch as Gonzales walks over and says, "You see that? Amish jumped forty feet off Jericho Tower."

Sergeant Hanson slaps his watch back in his pocket and spews, "We would have had a new squad record, but it doesn't count."

"What? Why not?"

"Cuz that idiot didn't use a rope."

Gonzales rolls his eyes and says, "Crapola."

Sergeant Hanson watches as Noah and his squad celebrate in the distance. He cups his hands and yells, "Amish! Get yer sorry ass over here!"

Back in the barracks, on his hands and knees, Noah is scrubbing the floor again. Sergeant Gonzales walks up behind him and says, "Hochstetler, Sergeant Hanson wants to see you in his office… now!"

"Aye, aye, Sergeant Instructor." Noah straightens his uniform and heads for Sergeant Hanson's office. When he arrives, he raps on the half-open door. Hanson looks up and waves Noah inside. The sergeant removes his reading glasses, taps his pen on his desk, and grumbles, "That was some stunt you pulled jumping off that tower like that."

"Sorry, Sergeant Instructor. I didn't know jumping off was against the rules."

"Cost us an obstacle course squad record."

"It won't happen again."

"You're right, it won't. I'm recommending you for a general discharge due to insubordination."

"Insubordination? All I did was jump off the tower."

"I can turn it into a dishonorable discharge if you want."

He knew a dishonorable discharge was the worst punishment a soldier could get other than a court-martial. Was jumping off a wall really that bad? Did he want to kick him out of the Army because he had German blood?

Desperate, Noah says, "I only have a few weeks left. I wanna be a soldier. I got nowhere else to go."

"Go home. Be a farmer."

"Can't you give me another chance?"

The sergeant stares at Noah. "How bad you want it, Amish?"

"How bad do I want what Sergeant Instructor?"

"To stay in the Army?"

"I'll do whatever it takes."

"Shut the door."

Noah shuts the door as Sergeant Hanson stands up and points at Noah. "Okay. Drop your pants."

"What?"

"You heard me. Everything down… skivvies too."

"Nae. You can't make me do that."

"I can make you do whatever the hell I want. You wanna stay in the Army or go home? The choice is yours."

Noah's eyes darken as he loosens his belt. He had never been so scared in his life. Is this happening? Maybe the sergeant's only joking. Maybe he wants to see if he will obey orders, no matter what he asks him to do. His heart races as he lowers his pants and the sergeant starts his way.

Noah exits Sergeant Hanson's office tightening his belt with a scowl. As he passes the scrub bucket, he gives it a swift kick and water flies everywhere.

Angry and confused, Noah heads to the empty shower room and removes his clothes. He turns on the water and furiously scrubs his entire body with a large bar of soap. Not satisfied, he slaps his hand against the wall, leans over, and cries. Who can he tell? Sergeant Gonzales won't do anything. How about his hippie friends, Bill and Dick? What would they do? They have their selves to worry about. Maybe he should run away like the two cowards in the books Mavis Thompson gave him. Still not sure what to do, Noah towels off and stares at his reflection in the mirror. Disgusted by what he sees, he slaps the glass with his towel and growls, "Nie wieder! 'Ich will do to him as he hath done to me'."

Noah is lying on the top of his bunk staring at the ceiling. He feels damaged, unloved, and worthless. Why did he let the sergeant do what he did to him? Somehow, when he was growing up, he thought women were the only ones who got raped. Would he ever get over the shame he was feeling right now? For the first time in his life, he wanted to kill himself. He sits up, grabs his pillow, tosses it across the room, and screams, "AHHH!"

His bunkmate, resting underneath him, kicks Noah's mattress. "Settle down up there, tiger! You're gonna get yourself shit canned."

Noah hops out of his rack, retrieves the pillow, climbs back in his bunk, and buries his face in his blanket.

Two days pass and the members of the 4th platoon are seated on their bunks and footlockers cleaning their M-16s. Satisfied his rifle is fit for inspection, Noah lays it down, opens his footlocker, removes a bayonet, and polishes it with a rag.

An hour later, members of the 4th platoon stand at attention with their rifles tight against their legs. Now in his dress uniform, heavily decorated with medals and ribbons, Sergeant Hanson yells, "Present arms!" The recruits present their rifles and sergeants Hanson and Gonzales walk down the line inspecting their weapons and uniforms. When Hanson reaches Noah, he grabs his rifle and looks it over carefully. He smiles, "Exceptional. Good job, Hochstetler."

Having finished the inspection, Sergeant Hanson pulls Sergeant Gonzales aside and whispers in his ear. Gonzales turns to the men and yells, "Fall out! Smoke'em if you got'em!"

Sergeant Hanson and several men head back to the barracks, while others, including Noah, Bill, and Dick light their cigarettes. Still not used to smoking, Noah coughs as Sergeant Gonzales approaches the threesome and says, "Sergeant Hanson wants to see you in his office, Amish."

The ex-hippies look at each other, not sure what to think. Finally, Bill says to Noah, "That asshole still giving you a hard time?"

Dick turns to Bill. "Didn't you hear Sergeant Hanson praising Amish here for his clean rifle? I used the word exceptional. I think they're buddies now."

"Go to hell!" Noah drops his cigarette and stomps it out.

He hurries off and Dick hollers, "We'll catch you later!"

Bill shakes his head. "You don't know when to shut up?"

"Peace out. I was trying to be nice. Amish has some anger issues."

Noah stands frozen in front of Sergeant Hanson's closed office door. He finally raps on it and from inside he hears, "Come in."

He enters and stands at attention. "You wanted to see me… Sergeant Instructor?"

Noah, who is holding a bucket, reaches behind his back with his other hand and grips the handle of the bayonet that is lodged in the back of his pants. Hanson grins. "What's with the bucket?"

Noah doesn't answer, so the sergeant walks past the recruit and shuts the door. When he turns back, Noah drops the bucket and thrusts his bayonet deep into the gut of the sergeant. He pulls the eight-inch blade out and buries it fully into Hanson's stomach two more times. The stunned sergeant groans as blood darkens the front of his shirt and oozes from his mouth. Slowly, he sinks to his knees in front of Noah. The recruit steps aside and the molester collapses face-first on the floor.

Not far from a military guard house, Noah kneels on the ground in front of a twelve-foot chain-linked fence with razor wire on top. When he's sure no one is watching, he uses his bayonet to dig under the barrier. When the hole is deep enough, he crawls under it and runs off.

It's almost noon when Sergeant Gonzales raps on Sergeant Hanson's office door. There's no response, so he takes a moment and walks inside. "Sarge, you going to chow or not?" Gonzales steps back when he sees his colleague hanging from a coat hook on the wall next to several glass-framed certificates of achievement and commendation. Hanson, who has been gutted like a pig, has a scrub bucket next to him that is filled with his blood and intestines. Gonzales leans over and starts to throw up, but manages to back out of the room and stagger into the corridor of the barracks. A few recruits stare at him, while others mind their own business as the sergeant hurries off.

Chapter 9

A Greyhound bus is headed north as Noah, still in his blood-splattered army fatigues, looks out the window thinking about how only hours earlier he had butchered a human being. He had never even hit another person, so knew he was in deep shit now. One moment the sergeant was alive and the next he was dead. Not only was his dream of being an Army officer over, but he knew it was just a matter of time until the authorities caught him and sent him straight to prison. He figured he'd never see his family again or Amish country for that matter. He had heard they sent Army criminals to Fort Leavenworth, Kansas. Would they execute him? Do they still hang people in this country? Maybe the Army would put him in front of a firing squad or strap him into an electric chair. He tried to imagine what it would feel like to have an electric current go through his body until his heart stopped. He had touched an electric fence when he was eight and it wasn't too bad. Yes, he wanted to be electrocuted. As he continued to think about dying, he stared out the bus window watching the farms go by. He wondered what his family was doing right now. Had someone already told them what he did? No, his folks didn't have a phone. Would the whole Amish community find out? What would Malachi think? Would his father tell Eli what he had done? Then he remembered why he left. Home is where everything remains the same and you are never forgiven.

Seated across from him is an elderly man in a worn-out dark blue suit, accessorized by a misshaped grey fedora hat. He clears his throat, looks at Noah, and says, "See you're in the Army. Is that Vietnam blood on your uniform."

"Cut myself shaving."

Noah tightens his lips and glares at the old man, who doesn't give up. "See a lot of action over there?"

Thinking he could shut the old man up, he says, "Nae, das habe ich nicht."

As the bus slows on the outskirts of the small town of Blairsville, Georgia, the old man tries again. "Die bushaltestelle… bus stop." Noah gives him a curious look and the old man smiles. "Studied German in high school but never got to use it much. Was in the Army myself, World War Two. Never left the Atlanta supply depot. Killed a deer once. Not the same as shooting at some fella firing back at you, but at least it was something."

The bus stops at the Blairsville Bus Station and the old man stands up and grabs his tattered leather suitcase. "This is me. Where you headed?"

Noah reluctantly answers. "Philadelphia… maybe Canada."

"Canada? Never been myself. See any of those draft dodgers, give them hell for me. Damn, cowards." The man tips his hat and heads for the front of the bus. "Been nice talking with you." He steps aside when a one-legged soldier, dressed in Marine Corps fatigues, hops on the bus and makes his way past the old man and down the aisle.

The old-timer exits the bus and Noah watches as the amputee balances his duffel bag in one hand and his crutch in the other. The twenty-something takes the seat vacated by the old duffer. As he settles in his seat, he turns and sees Noah staring at him. "Marines. Battle of Khe Sanh, E Company. You?"

Noah hesitates and says, "Army, Fort Benning, C Company."

The veteran snorts, "You a newbie?"

"Just got out of boot camp."

"Lucky you're joining now. Had no choice. It was either jail or the Marines. Should have gone to jail. At least I'd have two legs."

"I joined to see the world."

The Marine laughs. "Why? Ya think they were gonna send ya to some damn beach in Hawaii? All I saw were rice patties and a jungle full of monkeys, rats, and pissed-off gooks."

"How did you lose your...?"

"Land mine. Hadn't been there a month. Would've bled to death, but the big kaboom cauterized my stump. Doctor pulled leg bones out of my ass with a pair of pliers. All I got was a dumb-ass purple medal that I lost in a poker game… and a new left-footed boot. Do yourself a favor and get out when you can. Your dead body in some black bag ain't gonna change a thing."

He shifts in his seat. "I'll keep that in mind."

Noah is having a disturbing dream in which he sees himself sitting at a kitchen table watching Sergeant Hanson hand out Christmas presents to his wife and two kids. He groans and sits up. He wipes the moisture from his window and watches as the bus slows to a stop at the Philadelphia terminal. He looks around and notices the wounded soldier is gone as he gathers his belongings.

Walking down the street, Noah looks around trying to get his bearings. He spots a gypsy cab, signals the driver and a yellow Ford Galaxie pulls up. He climbs inside and sees that the man's nametag reads, Pavan Singh. He quickly finds out that Pavan has a combo Philly-East Indian accent, when the driver says, "Where do you wish to go soldier?"

"North… county road 7. I think I can show you how to get there."

Pavan snickers. "Dat would be good. I've never traveled to dat place before."

Thirty minutes later, the cab turns off the main highway and down county road 7. Pavan slows to a stop, and Noah gets out. To his right in an open field is a burnt-out area where he torched the Chevy Impala weeks earlier. He turns to the driver. "I'm going to need a ride back to Philadelphia."

"I can wait all day as long as you pay."

Noah nods and makes his way to the white rock where he buried his belongings ten weeks earlier. He pulls up his pant leg and removes the duct tape and the bayonet stuck to it. Pavan watches as Noah uses the weapon to dig under the rock. After he uncovers his special quilt and duffel bag, he tosses the bayonet into an open field and heads back to the cab.

Now in the back seat, Noah stares straight ahead thinking about what is next. He can't stay in Philadelphia, can't go home, and the money he dug up won't last long. Pavan looks in his rearview mirror, sees the duffel bag at his passenger's side, and raises his eyebrows. "You a bank robber?"

"I'm Amish. We don't rob banks." Under his breath he whispers, "But I did kill someone."

Pavan says, "You look to be in the Army."

"I just got out."

"Army... Amish? They don't go together."

"You're right about that."

Pavan pulls up to the Philadelphia bus depot and Noah pays him. On the street, he looks around to see if he is being followed and ducks inside the terminal. He finds an empty spot at the end of a bench and puts his bag and quilt between his feet. Bored, he picks up an abandoned newspaper, thumbs through it, and finds a small banner on the back page that reads: *Fort Benning Army Sergeant Killed in His Own Office.* After he reads the article, he stands up and stuffs the newspaper in a nearby trash can. He sits back down and looks at a young black man across from him wearing torn blue jeans, a hooded grey sweatshirt, Converse basketball shoes, and a dirt-stained Phillies baseball cap. The young man sees Noah staring at him and frowns. "What you lookin' at boy scout?"

Noah gets straight to the point. "U.S. Army… We're about the same size. I need a change of clothes. Give you fifty dollars for what you're wearing."

"You crazy, man? You ain't got fifty bucks to pay."

Noah reaches into his bag and counts out fifty dollars. He waves the cash at the skeptic. "Money I earned taking care of pigs,"

"Pigs? We talking ham and bacon pigs… or something else?"

"Ja, the first kind."

The young man takes his time. "You for real, man?"

"For real."

"If I give you my shit, what am I gonna wear?"

"We'll trade. What I got on is an army-issued uniform and boots. You can sell them. Make more money. We can change in the bathroom."

"What's all that shit on your shirt?"

"Blood, but it'll wash off."

"Ya kill somebody or something?"

"You want the money or not?"

They stand up, stare at each other, and head for the restroom. The black man whispers, "Better not be no funny shit when we get in there. Got me a knife and I ain't afraid to use it."

"How much do you want for the knife?"

He slaps his back pocket. "No way. Chased off three gangbangers and a pissed-off whore with this blade."

Back on the bus headed north, Noah sits alone in the back with his duffel bag at his feet and his quilt on his lap. The depot man's clothes are a fit, but the basketball shoes are two sizes too big. A white-haired lady sitting across the aisle looks at his quilt and smiles. "Bet your mother made that for you."

Noah suddenly has an urge to tell a lie like his friend Malachi and says, "Stole it from a homeless lady before I got on this bus." The woman cringes and looks away. Feeling guilty, Noah grins and apologizes, "I was only joking. Guess that wasn't very funny was it?"

"No, it wasn't."

"You're right. Mei mother made it for me before I left home."

The woman gives Noah a make-up smile. "I see. Well, what is your final destination?"

"Canada."

"How nice. I'm going to Canada as well. My sister lives in Toronto. What takes you there?"

As Noah thinks about the question, he wonders why he always gets stuck sitting next to some old person who wants to know everything about him. He thinks about telling the lady to mind her own business, but his Amish respectability kicks in and he says, "I want to be a Royal Canadian Mounted policeman."

The woman dabs her nose with an embroidered handkerchief and smiles. "Don't you need to be a Canadian citizen to do that?"

Noah hesitates. "You're probably right. Guess I'll do something else for a while."

"We change buses in Buffalo before we cross into Canada."

Noah shrugs. "Ja, I heard that."

The lady turns quiet, so he looks out the window and sees a farmer on a tractor cutting alfalfa in a large field. His mind drifts off as he thinks about his days on the farm. All the hard work and the smell of pigs didn't seem so bad anymore… and maybe his father wasn't so horrible after all. Working in the fields, marrying a local girl, and following the Amish ways would certainly be better than rotting in a prison cell in Kansas. Of course, he knew none of that was possible now. He was a wanted man, a killer, and a fugitive who was about to leave the only country he had ever known.

Hours later, the bus comes to a stop at the Buffalo depot. Noah and several other passengers secure their belongings and get on another bus headed for Canada. As luck would have it, Noah finds an open seat next to the white-haired lady again. He gives her a courtesy smile, turns away, and stares out his frost-covered window. Then he lays his head back and closes his eyes.

He's about to fall asleep when he hears the woman softly sing, "Oh Canada! Our home and native land. True patriot love thou dost in us command." She pauses, taps her knee, and says, "That's all I remember." Noah doesn't respond, so she removes a ball of yarn from her bag and begins to knit.

An hour later, the forty-passenger vehicle with Trans Canada Bus Company on its side, stops at the border crossing just north of Buffalo as Noah wakes from his nap. The bearded driver, Kyle Swenson, opens the bus door and looks back at his passengers. "Should only take a few minutes, folks. Get out your IDs and hide all those fruits and vegetables."

Kyle laughs at his joke as a Canadian border patrol officer comes on board. As he walks down the aisle checking people's IDs, Noah removes his birth certificate and social security card from his bag. When the officer reaches Noah, he holds out his hand like he's expecting a tip. "Identification." Noah gives the pale-skinned man his birth certificate and social security card. The officer looks them over and hands them back. "I need a photo ID."

Noah reluctantly reaches into his duffel bag, pulls out his military ID card, and hands it to him.

The officer looks at it carefully. "This is you, eh?"

Noah removes his cap. "Had hair 'til the Army took it all."

The officer tightens his eyes and continues to look at the card. "This is a military ID. You still in the Army?

"No, sir. I got an honorable discharge last week."

"How long will you be in Canada?"

"I don't know... a few days."

The officer stiffens. "The thing is I need to know exactly how long you're planning to stay."

"Okay, four days."

He gives Noah a curious look and starts to give him back his ID, but pulls it back and looks at it again. "Be right back."

The man heads to the front of the bus and the white-haired woman turns and says, "Did you do something wrong?"

Noah doesn't respond as he watches the officer lean over and say something to Kyle loud enough for everyone to hear. "Just be a minute and you can be on your way." The officer exits the bus and walks into the border station.

Noah looks out the bus window and watches as the officer speaks to a male counterpart inside, who immediately makes a phone call. Noah grabs his duffel bag and quilt, removes his pistol from the bag, and walks to the front of the bus. He points the gun at Kyle as several people begin to whisper. He turns to them and lowers his weapon. "Everyone stay calm. I've never done this before."

The passengers talk amongst themselves as Noah focuses on the wide-eyed bus driver. Kyle takes a series of deep breaths and says, "Put that gun away before you hurt someone."

"Listen. Start the bus. We're going to Canada... now."

"Sure, you wanna do this, son?"

"I'm not your son. Don't make me shoot you."

Kyle starts the bus and drives slowly toward the border crossing. Royal Canadian Mounted Police Officer, Morgan Winston, seated in his patrol car drinking coffee, looks out his window at the slow-moving bus and waves it through the open gate ahead.

Noah moves closer to Kyle. "Wave back at him and pick up the pace." Kyle waves at Sergeant Winston and merges onto the Canadian highway on the other side of the border.

The bus picks up speed, while back at the patrol station, the border officer hurries out the door with his gun drawn. He looks for the bus, doesn't see it, and runs back inside.

Still standing next to the driver with his gun pointed down, Noah sees an approaching sign: *Queen Elizabeth Way*. Passengers continue to talk amongst themselves as a young girl in pigtails removes a camera from her purse and takes Noah's photo. The reluctant hijacker hurries over, grabs the camera, and puts it in his duffel bag. The girl whines, "Hey mister, my grandmother gave me that camera for Christmas."

In the distance, Noah hears the faint sound of a siren, so he points his gun at Kyle and says, "Speed it up. You're going too slow." The bus accelerates as Noah checks the rearview mirror expecting to see a police car. As the sun disappears behind a cloud and it starts to snow, Noah sees a gravel road in the distance and points. "Take a right on that road up ahead."

Kyle tightens his lips. "I don't think that's a good idea."

"Do what I say."

The bus driver turns off the highway and onto a roughly-graded gravel road. A minute later, Noah looks back and sees the flashing lights of two police cars as they speed down the highway past the turn-off. As the road narrows, Noah looks out the window and grimaces. "Stop the bus!" Kyle breaks to a stop and Noah assesses the situation. Up ahead he sees a forest of pine trees and a small wooden bridge. He turns to Kyle and says, "Give me your coat."

Kyle leans forward and Noah removes the driver's parka from the back of his seat. The driver rolls his eyes and says, "Come on. The company gave me that for ten years of exemplary service."

Noah ignores him and grabs a stocking cap off the head of a bald man sitting in the second row. Then he hollers, "Gloves. Who has a pair of gloves?" No one responds, so he waves his gun at a few front-row passengers, and the bald man hands over his gloves. Noah reaches into his bag and pulls out some money. He hands Kyle a twenty-dollar bill and the bald man a ten. He puts on his new winterwear and turns back to Kyle. "This bus has a spare tire, right?"

"Yeah, what you want with that?"

Noah opens the bus door and steps outside with his belongings. He aims his gun at the left front tire and fires. It hisses as Noah waits for it to deflate.

Satisfied, he runs down the gravel road until he gets to the wooden bridge. Halfway across, he looks back at the bus. He pauses and leaps off, his arms flailing. He lands on the bank next to a large stream of water, brushes himself off, and runs for a grove of pine trees still clutching his duffel bag and quilt.

Back at the bus, the white-haired lady turns to the man across from her and says, "That young man sure loves that quilt his mother made for him."

Chapter 10

Ten miles north of the Canadian border centered on a narrow hiking path, Noah jogs through the forest dodging low-lying tree limbs and jumping over jagged rocks. Overheated by Kyle's oversized coat, Noah removes his cap and gloves and puts them in his pockets. He wipes the sweat from his forehead and starts running again.

As he ducks under tree limbs and hops over rocks, all he can think about is how the laws he had broken were starting to add up… he had killed a man, deserted from the Army, illegally crossed the border, and kidnapped a bus full of people. And to make things worse, he had no idea where he was going.

At the bus, Kyle and three male passengers stare hopelessly at the right front tire. A police car arrives with lights flashing and parks behind the bus. RCMP officer, Sergeant Morgan Winston, steps out of his vehicle and studies the scene. The tall slender man, dressed in a red serge tunic, midnight blue riding britches with a yellow stripe, and brown leather boots, strides over to the bus. Kyle sees the officer approaching and throws up his hands.

Sergeant Winston removes his revolver from his holster and addresses the four men. "What do we have here? The man who hijacked this bus… is he inside?"

Kyle steps forward. "Nah. He stole my coat, shot this here tire, and ran off." He points. "That way. He disappeared off that bridge."

"What? He jumped off the bridge?"

"Yeah, that's what I said. What am I gonna do here? I ain't got what it takes to change this tire.

"Just sit tight. I'll radio for some help. After he jumped, did you see what direction he was headed?"

"Nope, but he had himself a red duffel bag, some kind of blanket, and my damn coat."

Morgan stares at the bridge and heads back to his patrol car.

As Noah fast walks through the trees, he trips over a gnarly root and falls face down on the forest floor. He lays flat on the ground trying to catch his breath. He recovers, sits up, grabs his belongings, and heads for the sunlight breaking through the aspens ahead.

A few minutes later he emerges from the trees and sees smoke rising from a farmhouse chimney in the distance. When he reaches the modest homestead, he spots a corral filled with a dozen six hundred-pound Yorkshire pigs. He sniffs the air, leans over the railing, and snorts, "Hey, pig, pig, pig, pig!"

The barn door opens and Cyrus Middleton, a hefty bearded man in a long denim coat, knee-high rubber boots, and a dirty red toque exits with a pitchfork in his left hand. The forty-five-year-old farmer stares at Noah and shifts his eyes to the interloper's duffel bag and quilt. "What you doing on my land, boy?"

Caught off guard, Noah says, "Ich bin veloren."

The farmer lifts his chin. "Say that again… in English."

"I'm lost. I got turned around a few miles back in the trees. I'm trying to find my way back to a main road."

"You German or American?"

"American. I'm from Pennsylvania."

"Why you talking like a German?"

"I do that when I get nervous. I used to be Amish."

"Niagara Falls is twenty miles south and Toronto a hundred. Be best if you head back to the border highway. Why you out here by yourself, anyway?"

"Had the bus driver drop me off. Figured I'd hike around a while but lost my way."

"You ain't so smart, are ya?"

"I know and it's getting dark. Think I could spend the night in your barn. Can pay if you want."

"Listen, Yank. This ain't no Holiday Inn. Not one of them draft dodgers are ya?"

"Vietnam is over. I'm here to see Canada."

"Not a good idea traipsing around the country this time of year. Likely to freeze to death."

"I had it in my head to enjoy the journey, not just the destination. I'm planning to get on another bus in Niagara Falls." Noah waits as the farmer's eyes soften.

"All right. But you sleep in my house, so I can keep an eye on you. Got a room with no bed, but have me one them sleeping bags you can use. Sally Ann will fix up some grub when the time is right."

"Sally Ann? Your wife?"

"Hired gal... lives with me full-time. Won't be talking to you though. She's a mute." Cyrus grins, revealing two missing teeth. The huge man reaches out his oversized hand and Noah shakes it. "Cyrus Middleton."

"Jacob... Jacob Smith."

"Cyrus studies Noah's coat. "Your coat says you're Kyle."

"I bought it from the bus driver."

Cyrus narrows his eyes. "Like I said, you stay, but don't be trying none of that traveling salesman shit with Sally Ann, eh, or I'll send you packing in the middle of the night."

Cyrus Middleton's house is cluttered with stacks of old magazines and newspapers, metal pots and pans, and worn furniture. Despite the clutter, the place has a cozy feel to it. The farmer and Noah sit at opposite ends of a small kitchen table drinking coffee. Having shed his coat, Cyrus is wearing bib overalls and a tattered white Henley shirt. Even with the heat from the wood-burning fireplace, both men still have their stocking caps resting on their heads.

From the kitchen, Sally Ann bangs a pot with a spoon. The pretty eighteen-year-old with long brown hair and perfect teeth glares at Cyrus and he removes his cap. He tosses it on the floor, revealing his long and tangled hair. Noah takes the hint, removes his stocking cap, and puts it on his lap. Sally Ann studies the visitor's cropped hair and smiles.

Minutes later, she drops a second porkchop on Noah's plate. She tries to give him another helping of boiled potatoes, but he holds up his hand. "Nae, danke. I'm stuffed." Noah belches and Sally Ann and Cyrus stare at him. Noah blushes and says, "That's how the Amish say thank you."

Sally Ann smiles a little too long and Cyrus glares at her. She notices, turns away, and goes back to the kitchen. The farmer winks at Noah and whispers, "Being with her is real quiet. Not fond of women talk anyway."

Noah looks over at Sally Ann and raises his voice. "Thanks, Sally Ann! That meal captured the zeitgeist of the Canadian countryside!"

Cyrus raises up. "What the hell's zeitgeist?"

"You know, the spirit of a place."

Sally Ann turns, grins, and signs: "You're welcome."

Cyrus licks his thumb. "She says you're welcome. And no reason to yell. Ain't nothin' wrong with her ears."

"Okay. Right."

The farmer stands up and yawns. "Going to bed. Got me some deep plowing to do in the morning."

Noah scoots back from the table. "I can help you out tomorrow… pay you back for my stay. I know pigs."

Cyrus leans against the back of his chair. "What ya mean you know pigs?"

"I helped my father raise Yorkshires and worked for a pig farmer who had forty Durocs."

"Heard Duroc meat is pretty tasty."

"You heard right. Tender too."

"Don't ya gotta get yourself to Niagara Falls?"

"I'm in no hurry."

"You willing to shovel shit out of a pig pen?"

"Sure. I'm an expert mist scooper."

"And maybe you can make some sense out of my barn."

"I can do that too." Cyrus and Noah don't notice as Sally Ann looks down at the sink full of dishes and smiles.

Cyrus points to the back of the house. "Put the bag in there. Not much of a room, but you'll only be sleeping."

In a small storage room, Noah lies on the floor in a sleeping bag staring at the ceiling. He reaches into his duffel bag, removes his radio, and tries to find a station. All he hears is static, so he tosses it back in his bag. He pulls his quilt up to his chin, closes his eyes, and his mind starts to wander.

Why was he staying in some farmer's house in southern Canada? Where will he end up tomorrow? Will the authorities find his footprints in the nearby forest? And why did he tell Cyrus his name was Jacob Smith? Maybe he should leave now. His thoughts start to blur as he drifts off to sleep.

Noah sits up when he hears someone crying at the other end of the house. He climbs to his feet and tiptoes into the darkness of the living room. He steps back when he sees a bedroom door open and Cyrus leaving in his gray thermal long johns. Behind him, through the open door, he sees Sally Ann in bed crying with her arms folded across her chest. Cyrus notices Noah and shuts the door. They stand frozen in the dark until the farmer growls, "Go back to your room. She just had a bad dream."

It's early morning and Noah is in Cyrus's pig pen shoveling manure into an oversized wheelbarrow. He wipes the sweat from his brow, looks to his left, and sees Sally Ann exit the house with what looks like a cup of coffee. Adorned in a solid white calico dress, she starts toward him but stops and looks at the field across the dirt road, south of the farm.

In the distance, Noah sees Cyrus seated on a faded green John Deere tractor. Behind it is a twelve-foot tandem disc tearing up the dark brown soil.

When Sally Ann reaches the visitor, she offers him the cup and he takes it. He smiles and says, "Danke."

She starts to leave but Noah puts his hand on her shoulder. "Everything all right? I heard you crying last night."

Sally Ann tightens her lips.

"None of my business, but you don't have to let him do that."

She signs something to him and he shakes his head and says, "Sorry, I don't know what..." She starts to cry and before Noah can react, Sally Ann hurries back to the house.

Noah is finishing his work in the pig pen when he sees a patrol car approaching in the distance. He hops over the fence, ducks into the barn, and stands against the wall as the driver parks in front of the barn.

The officer steps out of his vehicle, looks around, and heads for the Middleton house. He climbs the porch steps, knocks, and waits patiently until Sally Ann opens the door. He hands her his card and says, "Sorry to bother you, Ma'am. I'm Sergeant Morgan Winston, RCMP. Does anyone live here with you? Sally Ann points at Cyrus, who is still plowing at the far end of the field.

"That your husband? Father?"

She signs something and points to her open mouth. Sergeant Winston takes a small step back. "All right then. I didn't know you were... Anyway, we're looking for a Noah Hochstetler. He's an American, eh." He pulls a piece of paper from his pocket with Noah's photo on it and shows it to her. "The thing is, he's the prime suspect in the murder of a man in Fort Benning, Georgia. Yesterday, he took a bus hostage and vacated it ten miles from here."

Sally Ann shrugs her shoulders, suggesting she doesn't know anything.

"Wouldn't be inside, would he Ma'am?"

She signals him to look for himself, so he removes his pistol and walks into the house, Sally Ann close behind.

Five minutes later, Winston and Sally Ann exit, and the officer looks at the barn. "How about the barn? Been in there lately?"

Sally Ann shrugs again. Winston walks towards the barn and removes the gun from his holster again. He makes his way inside and looks the place over. When he sees a pile of hay, he grabs a pitchfork and pokes it gently like he's afraid he might stab someone. A chicken roosting nearby, flies up, startling him. Satisfied, he vacates the barn and starts for his vehicle.

Before he opens his car door, Winston hollers at Sally Ann, standing in front of the house. "Sorry for the bother Ma'am, but if you see the man, don't approach him, and give me a call, eh." She waves and Winston starts his car and drives off.

That evening, Noah and Cyrus are seated at the dinner table finishing their Shepherd's Pie when Sally Ann, now wearing a pink cotton dress, walks over and gives them each a large piece of pie.

Noah sits up. "Wow! What do we have here?"

Cyrus's eyes sparkle. "Saskatoon pie. Berries grow wild around here. Pick'em myself."

"Looks awful good, Sally Ann."

Cyrus turns to her. "Did I see a car parked by the barn this morning?"

Sally Ann signs him a brief message and turns away.

Cyrus eyes Noah. "How about you? You see anyone?

"I was in the barn most of the day."

"Yeah, I checked it out. Cleanest it's been since I built it. Huh, I was at the far end of the field, but I swear I saw a car. Eyes ain't what they used to be. Might have been someone lost or something like you was."

Noah changes the subject. "Almost finished. Give me a couple more hours in the morning."

"Stay longer if ya want. Got a few more odd jobs if you're up to it."

"No, I should be going. Do you mind if I sleep in the barn tonight?

"Why would you wanna do that?"

"Kind of reminds me of home."

Cyrus laughs. "Don't bother me none; gonna be cold as hell out there tonight."

"I'll be all right. Think I'll head out there. I'm kind of tired."

"Ain't no light. I'll fetch you a lantern."

"Not to worry. Got me a flashlight." Noah grabs his bag, puts on his coat, and picks up his quilt. He unzips the bag, finds his flashlight, and shows it to Cyrus.

Cyrus yawns. "There you go. Been a long day. Think I'm going to bed myself."

Noah grins. "See you in the morning. Danke for der dinner, das fräulein. Best meal I've had in a long time." Sally Ann smiles and Noah walks out the door.

Chapter 11

Noah shines his flashlight inside the barn looking for somewhere to sleep. He finds a place not far from the door, fashions a bed out of loose hay, opens his duffel bag, and removes his pistol. He buries it under a pile of hay where he's about to bed down. He turns off his flashlight, lays back, and pulls his quilt to his chin.

He's almost asleep when he hears something. He grabs his flashlight, turns it on, and points it at the doorway. "Cyrus, that you?"

Sally Ann steps inside and Noah sits up. "Sally... what are you doing here?"

She holds up a fleece blanket.

"No, I'm good. Thanks for thinking of me, though." Noah looks at her face and sees that she's been crying. "Did he force himself on you again?"

She stares at Noah as he adds, "I know how you feel." Sally Ann lowers her head. "You don't have to stay here. Girl like you can find work anywhere."

She uses her index finger to point to her open mouth.

"You don't have to talk to get a good job. Most people would be better off if they didn't talk."

Sally Ann grins points at herself, and then at Noah. He squints and says, "What? You wanna sit with me?"

She scampers over and drops into the hay next to Noah. He slowly scoots away. "This isn't a good idea. Cyrus finds you here, he'll send me packing."

Sally Ann puts her index finger to her lips, lays next to him, and covers herself with her blanket. Noah stares at her, turns off his flashlight, and lays back in the hay. In the dark, he whispers, "Better not be here when he wakes up."

Noah and Sally Ann are sound asleep when a bright light shines in their eyes. They sit up and shade their faces, trying to see what is blinding them. Noah quickly realizes it's Cyrus standing in the barn doorway holding a kerosene lamp. The farmer glares at the young couple and growls, "What the hell you doing out here with my girl, Yank?" He shifts his attention to Sally Ann. "And you. You're a damn tramp just like your mother."

Noah spits hay from his mouth and says, "We didn't do anything. She came out here because she was afraid."

"Afraid of what?"

"You need to stay out of her room."

"You don't know shit."

"Yeah, it's time for me to leave."

Noah starts to stand up, but Cyrus grabs a nearby pitchfork and thrusts it at him. "Sit your ass down!"

"Just let me go my own way… Sally Ann too if she wants."

"Now ya wanna take my girl with ya. What other lies she been tellin'?"

"'Whoever walks in integrity walks securely, but he who makes his ways crooked will be found out.'"

"Whoever said that doesn't know shit!" Cyrus tosses his pitchfork but misses Noah's head by inches. With fire in his eyes, the farmer hustles to a work table and removes a hundred-pound cast iron anvil. He shuffles back and raises the makeshift weapon above his head with ease. As he prepares to toss it, Noah grabs his pistol from under the hay and shoots Cyrus square in the chest. The abuser drops the anvil at Noah's feet and his eyes widen as he looks at the blood covering his overalls. In slow motion, he sinks to the ground and stops breathing.

Sally Ann hurries over to Cyrus, falls to her knees, and starts to cry. "You... you… killed… him. You… killed my fa... father."

Noah looks confused as he turns to Sally Ann. "You can talk? He's your father?" Sally Ann turns away and Noah lowers his head.

Noah stands frozen in the doorway while Sally Ann sits in the hay still crying. "Why didn't you tell me Cyrus was your father?" She remains silent, so he continues, "You saw what happened. He would have killed me. I had no choice." Noah kneels next to her. "You can tell the authorities whatever you want, but I need your help. Will you help me?" Noah stands up and waits patiently until she joins him.

Noah looks around, grabs the pitchfork, and starts to cover the farmer with the hay he slept on. Sally Ann stops him, pulls a handkerchief from her father's pocket, and covers his face. When they finish burying Cyrus, Noah takes Sally Ann's hand and the young couple heads for the house.

Once inside, she helps him fill a large gunny sack full of food from the cupboard and refrigerator. Satisfied they have everything they need, the young couple hustles out of the house, Noah carrying his duffel bag, quilt, and a jug of water. A step behind, Sally Ann holds the gunny sack of food.

Noah looks around like he's waiting for a bus until Sally Ann points at Cyrus's tractor. Noah nods and they climb onboard. She takes a seat behind the steering wheel and manages to start the engine. Noah positions himself directly behind her, grips his belongings, and they drive off.

Motoring down the farm road at a moderate speed, Noah looks in the distance and sees a set of railroad tracks. He points and Sally Ann drives that direction. When they reach the tracks, they park the tractor and wait nervously.

An hour later, they see a freight train approaching. They hide behind the tractor as the locomotive slows for a crossing up ahead. When the train pulling fifty railcars, including flatcars, hoppers, and tankers slows down even more, Noah spots a boxcar with its door slightly open and points.

It picks up speed, so the runaways vacate their hiding place with their belongings in tow. As they run alongside the boxcar, Noah reaches out, slides the door open more, and tosses his belongings inside. Then he reaches back and grabs the gunny sack from Sally Ann. As he continues to run alongside the boxcar, he crawls halfway through the opening. His legs are dangling out of the doorway, when Sally Ann grabs Noah's shoe and it comes off in her hand. The train picks up speed again just as Noah manages to squeeze himself inside the car. He stumbles to his feet, turns back, and watches as Sally Ann waves goodbye with his basketball shoe. Tempted to jump out of the car, he looks in the distance and sees Cyrus's daughter climbing onto the tractor.

Sergeant Winston drives up to the Middleton farmstead. Before he can reach the house, the front door opens and Sally Ann walks out carrying her notebook. The mounted policeman meets her halfway across the yard and says, "Okay, I got a call from your neighbor. Take me to your father."

Sally Ann leads the way as they head for the barn. They walk inside and she points at the burial hay. The officer brushes enough of it away to reveal Cyrus's dead body. She hands Morgan her notebook and he reads it silently. "Says here your father found you and the fugitive in this barn. Your father then threw a pitchfork at him and was about to drop an anvil on his head so the fugitive shot him. Then he walked away in a direction you didn't see."

She nods yes and Morgan shows her a photo of Noah again. "And this is the man?"

She nods in agreement again.

"Same picture I showed you yesterday."

She lowers her head and Morgan continues. "Like I said, his real name is Noah Hochstetler and he's wanted for murder."

Sally Ann looks away, but the sergeant continues. "And you're sure he wasn't here when I stopped by the first time?"

Sally Ann raises her head and her eyes grow dark. "I'll take that as a no… for now." Winston reads a little more from the notebook. "You also claim here your father was molesting you, which is the reason you stopped talking… and that it got worse after your mother died."

Sally Ann tightens her lips and agrees with her eyes, so Morgan continues. "If you don't mind me asking, how did your mother die?"

Sally Ann pauses, points at the barn, and slowly runs her index finger across her throat.

"Your father killed her?"

Sally Ann bites her lower lip and the sergeant lowers his voice. "And you never told anyone? Miss Middleton, you didn't kill your mother did you?"

Sally Ann avoids the question, turns her head back, and looks at the officer defiantly. She grabs the notebook from Morgan, scribbles something, and hands it back.

The sergeant reads it out loud. "'I did what I did because my mother stood by and did nothing.'"

Morgan snorts. "One more question. Where is your mother buried?" Sally Ann looks at the pig pen and Morgan says, "In the barn?"

Sally Ann points at the pig pen.

"In that pigsty?"

Sally Ann takes a moment, grits her teeth, and makes a hand gesture mimicking a pig eating flesh and bones.

"Wait. The two of you fed her to the pigs. There's a lot to sort through here, Ma'am. Afraid you'll have to come with me to our headquarters in Niagara Falls."

Sally Ann starts to cry, signs something, and stutters, "She… she let him… rape me."

Morgan walks to his vehicle, opens the back door, and helps Sally Ann inside.

Chapter 12

Inside a Canadian Pacific Railway boxcar traveling west, Noah lies on his back staring at the ceiling, thinking about Sally Ann. He envisioned her running behind him, trying to keep up. Maybe at the last second, she had changed her mind and decided not to go with a pagan half-boy and half-man. How would things be different if she were with him right now? He figured she was already back at the farm telling the police that some drifter had killed her father and tried to kidnap her. Why wouldn't Sally Ann blame everything on him? They'd only known each other for two days. He thought she had feelings for him, but maybe she was only using him to get rid of her father. But why was she so upset when he shot the monster? He understood how you can hate someone and love them at the same time, but you can't go around shooting the people you hate, or you'll end up in prison or on the run like he was right now.

Noah's mind moves in another direction as he thinks about how in less than a week he had separated two men's souls from their bodies. What kind of lives would Sergeant Hanson and Cyrus Middleton have lived if he hadn't killed them? Were they in hell right now? Was he riding this graveyard train straight to hell himself? Would his victims be waiting for him when he got there?

Noah manages to calm himself down by rubbing his quilt against his face. For some odd reason, he began to imagine the smell of fermenting apples left on the ground as he and Malachi walked through his uncle's orchard months earlier. His stomach starts to grumble, so he removes a piece of Saskatoon berry pie from his burlap sack and eats it. He drinks from his water jug, lays back, stares at the ceiling, and thinks about what might lie ahead.

As the train rattles down the tracks, it slows to a stop not far from a small-town train station. Noah wakes when he hears the garbled sound of men talking. He sits up and watches as the freight car door slides open. He grabs his belongings and leans back as two men climb inside with their sleeping bags. They are both wearing tattered jeans, dirty flannel shirts, and skimpy coats not made for the Canadian winter cold. The older man, who looks to be in his late 40s, struggles to his feet and helps the twenty-something younger man up. Noah clicks on his flashlight and looks the intruders over. The older man snarls, "Turn that damn thing off! You're going to give us away!"

Noah turns off his flashlight. Tempted to remove the gun from his bag, he says, "Ich war here first. Find yourselves another place."

The boxcar jerks, the train picks up speed, and the older man chuckles. "Too late. We'll settle over here. Be no bother to you." The intruders drop down in the corner of the boxcar as Noah sits in the dark unsure what to do. The older man lights a match and holds it out. "Got any grub to share with two brothers who haven't eaten all day?"

"Maybe in der morgen."

"You German?"

"Amish."

"Huh."

The older man blows out the match, huddles with his partner, and moments later they begin to snore. Noah fashions his duffel bag as a pillow, pulls his quilt over his body, and drifts off.

The next morning, the boxcar door is wide open and the sun lights Noah and his new travel companions. Seated in the middle of the car, the three of them are eating the bread and ham Sally Ann packed before he boarded the train. The strangers finish and look at Noah. The older man says, "What else you got?"

Noah squeezes the bag shut. "That's all you get. I'm saving the rest for me. I don't know how long I'll be riding this train." Noah looks closely at the older man and sees that he has long greasy hair, dark brown eyes, and a dirt-stained face. He notices Noah staring at him, so he wipes his mouth, revealing his perfectly pearl-white teeth. He slicks back his hair, rubs his gray stubbled chin, and shakes his index finger at Noah.

"You must be a man of God."

"Why, because I'm Amish?"

"I have the gift of discernment. Plus, the spirit tells me you're an Old Testament believer, like Absalom and me. We're descendants of David and Bathsheba. Name's Solomon by the way, but you can call me Sol. Who might you be?"

Noah doesn't know why, but he gives the man his real name. "Noah… and how do you know what spirit is talking to you?"

Sol ignores what he said and smiles. "Noah, son of Lamech, ninth descendant of Adam."

"Nae. Noah, son of Moses."

"Kind of you to break bread with us, brother Noah.

Noah nods at Absalom, who has an odd smile, and says, "Not much of a talker is he?"

"That's cuz he ain't right in the head. Stayed too long in our mother's womb, but he's still a Son of David like me."

"Brother, huh?"

Sol nods yes as Absalom mumbles, "I ain't right in the head."

Sol grins. "Been meaning to ask. Why just the one shoe?"

"Long story, I don't wanna tell. So, your father's name is David?"

"It's Ralph, but Absalom and I started us a religion, the Sons of David."

"How do you start a religion?"

"God called me like he called Old Testament David, who was man after God's own heart just like me. 'And the Lord Almighty took David from the pasture and from following the flock and made him ruler over Israel.'"

"Only you're not David and this isn't Israel."

"But I am a Son of David."

"Your religion have any rules or words to live by?"

"Psalms, Proverbs, and Ecclesiastes."

"Written by David and his son Solomon."

"Praise be to God. You know the good book."

"Do you have any other believers?"

"Only Absalom and me, but you'd make three. How about it? You wanna be a Son of David? No cost."

"I'm already a member of the Whiskey Boys."

"Whiskey?"

Noah laughs. "Never mind. Like I said I'm Amish." He grabs his burlap food bag, duffel bag, and quilt. Then he stands up, takes a couple of steps back, and sits down again, his back against the box car door. "Gonna get me some sleep now."

As Noah rests, all he can think about are the strange men sharing his space. There was something odd about them. Maybe they are the run like he is and not who they are pretending to be. Maybe, they are waiting for a chance to steal everything he has. After leaving home, most of the people he has met after leaving home have a backpfeifengesicht… a slapable face.

It's the middle of the night and Noah is sound asleep under his quilt, his head resting on his duffel bag. In the corner of the boxcar, Sol strikes a match and sneaks over to Noah. He bends down, pulls a knife from his boot, and holds it behind his back. The match burns down and the flame scorches his finger. He drops the fire stick in some straw and he stomps it out.

Noah opens his eyes and sits up. "What's goin' on?"

"I'll take that food and fancy blanket." Noah doesn't react, so Sol flashes his six-inch blade. "You itching to be a sacrificial lamb? Hand it over."

Noah hands him his food bag but grips his quilt tightly. "You're not getting this."

Sol thrashes his knife downward as Noah scoots back, grabs his duffel bag, and pulls out his pistol. Before he can aim his gun, Sol kicks it out of his hand and jumps on top of him. As they wrestle, Sol drops his knife.

Sol gets the upper hand and puts his full weight on Noah's chest and stomach. Noah gasps for air and tries to push Sol away, but the oversized man grabs the knife from the floor and raises it above his head. "Prepare to meet your maker, son of Moses."

As Sol is about to plunge the knife, a gun goes off. Blood pours down from the side of Sol's head as he sinks to the boxcar floor. Noah looks up and sees Absalom holding his smoking gun.

Noah scoots away and stares at Absalom. "You shot your brother. I think he's dead."

Absalom looks down. "He's not my brother. God, what have I done?" Sol groans, flutters his eyes, and his vision of the outside world disappears.

As the two-engine Canadian Pacific Railway train continues west, it rounds a corner and approaches a snow-covered ravine.

The boxcar door opens and Noah and Absalom push Sol's lifeless and shoeless body out. Wrapped in a blanket, the body bounces once, rolls down the steep ravine, and into the valley below. Next to Sol's body are two notebooks.

In less than a week, Noah had watched three men die, two by his hand, and a third who would have killed him if not for the quick actions of the deranged man's brother. And why did Absalom choose to shoot his brother instead of him?

Noah's belief in God was at an all-time low. The little bit of faith his father had instilled in him started to fade after he killed Sergeant Hanson. Then everything went numb after he shot Cyrus Middleton. Despite the excuses he made for himself, the guilt was still there. He hadn't shot Sol, but he felt responsible for his death. There were moments when he didn't feel guilty at all because he figured all three men deserved to die. Then he realized it didn't matter what he thought. The police were going to find him and haul his ass to jail. And if there was a God, he knew He was waiting for him so he could send him straight to hell.

Wearing Sol's tattered shoes, Noah sits with the dead man's killer in the boxcar doorway. They are smoking cigarettes as large snowflakes filter an early morning rising sun. The young man, only a few years older than Noah, turns and says, "You're awfully quiet."

"Ich have a lot to be quiet about... So, your real name is Chad?"

"Chad Leroy Livingston... Toronto, Ontario. And you?"

"It's still Noah, Noah Hochstetler, Pennsylvania, Amish country."

"Good to know. We didn't get much of a chance to talk."

Noah grins. "Because you were simple-minded."

"Not simple-minded anymore. That was my asshole professor's idea."

"Sol was a professor?"

"Let's hold off on the questions for a while. I'm still trying to deal with the fact that I killed a man." Chad puts out his cigarette and Noah follows suit.

In the ravine below the tracks where Noah and Chad pushed Sol's body out of the boxcar an hour earlier, the blanket Chad and Noah wrapped Sol in opens and the Son of David flutters his eyes. The barefooted professor struggles to his feet. He grabs the two notebooks, picks up the blanket, and wraps it around his shoulders. Then he stumbles towards the rising sun in the ankle-deep snow.

Later that afternoon, the door is slightly ajar as Noah and Chad sit in the center of the boxcar staring at the passing pine trees and the wide-open dormant fields with patches of snow. Chad turns to Noah and says, "Kenneth Collins was my graduate school advisor from the University of Toronto, where I've been trying to finish a Master's degree in English. He had this hair-brained idea about writing the next great Canadian novel, a blend of Kerouac's *On the Road*, Steinbeck's *Travels with Charley*, and Twain's *Adventures of Huckleberry Finn*."

"Haven't read any of those books."

"Anyway, Dr. Collins got a year's sabbatical and convinced me to travel with him as his research assistant. Said it would be a social experiment and we'd travel across Canada for three or four months and create a story along the way."

"And what were you going to get out of it?"

"The self-indulgent bastard wanted me to take notes. His idea was I'd chronicle the travel experience part of the trip and turn it into my Master's thesis. I took the bait and not long after we left Toronto. Two weeks in, I realized he was a psychotic manipulator. He dominated all our conversations and made every decision." Chad pulls a journal from inside his shirt and hands it to Noah, who begins to thumb through it. "It's all in there."

"What's a Master's thesis anyway?"

"A meaningless research paper that graduate students have to write. Anyway, the first two months we rode in boxcars from Toronto to Vancouver looking for characters and stories for his book."

Noah hands the notebook back. "Characters like me?"

"Didn't get a chance to know you, but everyone else was the same... out of work, on the run from the law, or some poor homeless person going from town to town looking for the next handout."

"You two sure looked the part."

"That was his plan. Said we needed to dress and act like a couple of derelicts."

"A derelict?"

"Vagrant, bum, hobo, homeless person."

"Huh. That sounds like me."

"The plan was working until he turned evil. One day he woke up and said he was ready to make a change. He wanted to go from being the protagonist in his book to the antagonist. Said he was gonna raise hell until someone stopped him. He even bought himself a knife."

"Yeah, I saw the knife. And you went along with it?"

"I told him I'd had enough and wanted to go home, but he threatened to destroy any chance I had of finishing my degree.

Then he came up with an addition to his plan where he wanted to mix mind control with religion. Said he was going to act like a deranged lunatic and I needed to be his dim-witted brother. All part of his scheme to lure people in and convince them to join his new religion, The Sons of David."

Noah shares a thought. "Like my father always says, 'every man has evil in his heart. It's just a matter of whether he acts on it or not.'"

Chad wrinkles his nose. "You have evil in your heart?"

"More than my mother, less than my father. He thinks he's some sort of religious hero, but he's a mind-controlling villain like your professor."

"So, I take it that's your story. You left home because you couldn't get along with your father?"

"Started that way, but I also wanted to see the world. This is the first other country I've ever been to."

"Know what they say, Canada's just another Siberia with people who end sentences with eh." Chad studies Noah's face. "But I think you're on the run from something else. I can see it in your eyes."

Noah looks away and lifts his gunny sack. "We need to get off this train, so we can buy some food. What is the next city?"

"Regina. Not too far."

"When are du heading back east?"

"I don't know. There will be a lot of questions if I show up at the university without Dr. Collins."

"Could tell them he lost his mind and went his own way, which is kind of true."

"Only a matter of time until someone finds his body. We should have buried his ass."

"Leben ist kein ponyhof."

Chad grins. "Translation?"

"Life is no pony farm. Du can keep moving west with me if du want. Ich don't know where I'm going yet, but we can go there together."

Chad nods. "Let's talk about that after we find some food."

Chapter 13

As the train slows to a stop east of the Regina train depot, Noah and Chad hop out of their boxcar carrying all their possessions, including two sleeping bags. As they enter the capital of Saskatchewan, they immediately find Main Street. Chad scans the area, checking for a grocery store, and says, "Let's make it quick. Next train out of here isn't going to wait for us."

Noah spots a corner market and they hurry inside. Chad grabs a shopping cart. They begin to fill it with an assortment of canned and boxed food and other supplies. The grad student empties his pocket and says, "Twelve dollars. That's all Collins had in his pocket. How about you?"

Noah holds up a fistful of money and Chad smiles. "Okay, that helps. Keep shopping. I wanna use a real bathroom. Get some of those Frosted Flakes, eh."

Noah starts down the next aisle as Chad hurries to the front of the store. When he sees a bulletin board, a wanted poster catches his eye. He looks at it closely and realizes Noah's military ID photo is on it. He reads the description carefully as he rubs his forehead.

When he turns back, he sees the wanted man in the third aisle. Noah spots him, waves, and disappears around the corner. Chad stands frozen for a moment and then hurries out of the store.

Done shopping, Noah pushes his cart to the front of the store and looks for Chad. Not seeing him, he goes to the checkout counter and a young female clerk starts ringing up his groceries: a box of cookies, a box of cereal, four cans of soup, two tins of Spam, a dozen batteries for his flashlight, a box of matches, two coffee cups, a manual can opener, and a small cast iron frying pan.

The clerk smiles and says, "Don't you love Frosted Flakes? "They're grrreat!"

Noah ignores her as he continues to look for his companion.

"You know, like on TV."

Noah refocuses. "There was no TV in my house."

"Oh... looks like you're going camping, eh?"

"Du see the guy ich came in here with?"

"Yeah, he left a couple of minutes ago."

"Could du put it all in one bag?"

"You sure?"

"Ja, I got too much crap to carry."

"Like your accent. You Norwegian?"

"Nae, German."

She finishes bagging his groceries and Noah starts for the door. The clerk yells out, "I really like your blanket! I get off at four, eh."

Noah exits the store balancing his overstuffed grocery bag, duffel bag, his sleeping bag, and quilt. He doesn't see Chad, so he heads straight for the train tracks.

In a different boxcar, Noah stands in the doorway looking for Chad. The train lurches forward, so he lowers his shoulders and slides the door shut.

Where was Chad? Did he lose track of time? Did he hop on another train headed back to Toronto? Tempted to go and look for him, he thinks better of it, sits down on his sleeping bag, and wraps his quilt around his shoulders.

Inside the Regina police station, Chad sits across from Royal Canadian Mounted Police Sergeant Carl Everson, a portly man with an enormous red nose. Carl has a phone in his right hand while he studies Noah's wanted poster on his desk. He dials and waits for a response.

In Ontario, seated behind a black metal desk with a photo of Niagara Falls behind him, Sergeant Winston hears his phone ring and picks up the receiver. "Sergeant Winston, RCMP, Ontario division."

"Yes, this is Sergeant Carl Everson in Regina. I have a man in my office, Chad Livingston, who has identified the fugitive you've been looking for, Noah Hochstetler. Says he held him and his college professor hostage on a train headed this way. Said Hochstetler shot the professor and threw his body off the train a few miles west of Winnipeg, eh. I alerted the authorities there and they are looking for his body."

Back in Niagara Falls, Sergeant Winston sits up straight. "What about Hochstetler?"

"Well, after they got off here, Mr. Livingston made his escape. He thinks Hochstetler got back on the same train headed west."

"And this Livingston claims Hochstetler killed some professor?"

"He has all the details but again there is no body."

"If you don't mind, I'm going to drive your way. Been looking for this fellow for a while now. Can you keep the informant in the vicinity until I get there?"

On the other end of the line, Carl nods at Chad and says, "I can do that. You sure you want to come all this way?"

"Know what they say? We Mounties always get our man."

Lieutenant Everson chuckles. "Didn't know people still said that. Anyway, I'll alert the rail authorities in Calgary to be on the lookout for Hochstetler."

"Okay. See you when I get there."

Lieutenant Everson hangs up the phone and turns to Chad. "I need you to stay in Regina for a couple of days. The officer I spoke with wants to talk to you."

"Have a place where I can sleep?"

"Jail cell okay?"

"Yeah, no for sure. Has to be better than living in a boxcar."

Noah is sitting in the center of his private railroad car eating handfuls of Frosted Flakes out of the box with the aid of his flashlight. Satisfied, he lays back and aims his light at the ceiling. He hears a screech, so he points it at the top corner of the car where the sound is coming from.

He spots a Snowy Owl with black markings. The bird's head pivots a hundred and eighty degrees, revealing its bright orange tube-shaped eyes. He takes a moment and softly says, "Miss Thompson?"

He clicks off his flashlight but continues to watch the owl, whose eyes glow in the dark. Noah thinks about his last few days of school when Miss Thompson told him that an owl was a symbol of good luck and fortune and that the bird's purpose was to bring a person prosperity and wisdom. He had also read in a magazine that seeing one was a sign of bad luck. For once, Noah decided to go with Miss Thompson's interpretation. He'd had enough bad luck to last him a lifetime.

It's after midnight when the Canadian Pacific train pulls into the Calgary, Alberta rail station. Noah slides the boxcar door open. In the distance, he sees three police officers with two German Shepherds coming his way. As their flashlights flicker, signaling their approach, Noah grabs his belongings and jumps out of the boxcar. The officers don't see him as he hurries off into the night.

The next morning on the outskirts of Calgary, Noah stands on the side of an icy road holding his thumb out as snow-covered cars and trucks roar by him. The wind picks up as a paper cup rolls past him. Feeling defeated by the drivers' lack of sympathy, he sits down on his sleeping bag with his thumb still pointed west. The snow starts to fall again as an old Dodge pickup finally pulls over and a grey-haired woman waves him over. Noah grabs his belongings and runs for the rust-covered vehicle. When he looks at the woman through the driver's side window, she signals him to get in the bed of her truck.

Noah tosses his things in the back of the pickup and climbs aboard. With his back up against the cab, he smooths his sleeping bag out, sits on it, and huddles under his mother's quilt. As the blinding snow covers his tuque, he looks through the rear window, where he sees two small children pointing and laughing at him as a black and white Australian Shepherd pants.

When they reach the resort town of Banff, Alberta, the gray-haired woman pulls her truck over and Noah climbs out. He waves his thanks and she drives off. After he adjusts to his surroundings, he heads for the town's main street.

As Noah walks along, he's greeted by several citizens of Banff, a small tourist community nestled in the snow-capped Rocky Mountains and home to Canada's oldest national park.

People greet him with smiles and several men tip their hats. Noah already liked the place. It felt like home, even if there were no Amish people or Amish farms. Where should he go? Would the police be looking for him this far west? And how would he survive? He removes the remaining cash from his pocket and stares at it. Seven dollars. He spots a hardware store, walks inside, and two minutes later comes out with a box of bullets for his pistol.

Two days later at the Regina police station, Sergeant Everson, Sergeant Winston, and Chad are seated around a small table in the interrogation room. Sergeant Winston hands Chad back his notebook and says, "That's some story…. if it's true."

Chad tightens his lips. "Might've embellished a few things."

Sergeant Wilson shows Chad the wanted poster. "And you're sure this is him?"

Chad hands it back. "Positive. Even told me his real name."

"You remember how he was dressed?"

"Jeans, hooded grey sweatshirt, black toque, and a parka that had "Trans Canada Bus Company" printed on the back. Said he bought it from a bus driver named Kyle."

Sergeant Winston taps the table with his pen. "Appears he hasn't changed clothes since he crossed the border. Does he have anything unusual with him?"

"Food we bought, red duffel bag where he hides his gun, and some special blanket."

"Special?"

"Lots of colorful patches."

"You mean a quilt?"

"That's it. Guards it like it's made of gold."

Winston continues. "Do you have any idea where he's headed?"

"He didn't even know… just west."

Officer Everson says, "It appears you were on your way to being friends even after he shot the professor."

"No, I was faking it, so he wouldn't kill me. When I found out he'd killed two other people, I took a chance and ran off."

Sergeant Winston adds, "You told the sergeant here an argument broke out over food?"

"That, and Collins was angry because Noah didn't want to join his religious group."

"You mean your religious group don't you... The Sons of David?"

"I did go along with it, but I didn't have much choice."

"My guess is there's more to the story than what's in that notebook." Winston turns to Sergeant Everson. "As for Hockstetler, there's no question he killed his sergeant, but during the investigation, two recruits revealed that Hanson molested them. Then the other drill sergeant came forward and admitted seeing Hanson act inappropriately in his office with some other recruits but never reported it."

"Knew he was running from something or someone other than his father."

Sergeant Everson asks, "Who was the other man he killed?"

"Ontario farmer who was sexually abusing his daughter. Girl's mother found out, but she didn't put a stop to it, so the daughter decided to poison her instead of her father… with a piece of Saskatoon berry pie.

Chad shakes his head. "Sounds like a Greek tragedy."

"That's not all. With her father's help, they fed her mother to the pigs. Her old man was using the secret, so he could keep sexually abusing her and keep her quiet. Noah comes along, discovers the abuse, and calls him out on it. Farmer tries to drop an anvil on his head, so he shoots him."

Chad sits up straight. "Then we came along and he shot Professor Collins."

"Sure, you didn't shoot him?"

"What? Why would I do that?"

"Maybe Collins was abusing you."

"Sexually, no. Emotionally, yes."

"Would you be willing to take a polygraph test?" Chad stares at Sergeant Winston. "Do I need a lawyer?"

"I don't know. Do you?"

"I want to go back to Toronto."

"Headed that way. I'll take you with me."

Driving east, Sergeant Winston and Chad Livingston stare straight ahead as the windshield wipers try to keep up with the falling snow. Morgan breaks the silence. "Not good. Hope we can make it to Winnipeg before dark. I got a call before we left Regina and they still haven't found Collins' body. There's something that's been bothering me about your story."

Chad shifts in his seat. "What's that?"

"You said Collins was sitting on Noah when he shot him. But how could Noah grab the gun and shoot the professor in the back of the head if Collins was on top of him? Shooting a man in the back of the head from that angle is impossible. How do you explain that?"

"It was more on the side of the head. It happened so fast and it was kind of dark." They sit quietly as Chad looks out the passenger side window. Then he turns and says, "You're sure the men Noah killed were abusers?"

"For sure."

"So, he had a right to kill them."

"Could end up being justifiable homicide, but that's not my call."

"He was unlucky meeting up with those men. They were evil."

"Appears the professor was evil too."

"You have no idea."

"You wanna change your story?"

Chad lowers his head, looks out the window again, and slowly turns back. "It was me. I shot Collins, but he would've killed Noah if I hadn't. And it was my idea to toss him off the train."

"Why did you blame Noah?"

When I saw the wanted poster, I figured he had killed two other men, so blaming him for a third murder wouldn't make any difference."

Sergeant Winston pats Chad on the back as the young man lowers his head and slaps the window. "Am I going to prison?"

"Again, not my decision, but circumstances are in your favor if Collins was trying to kill Noah. They haven't even found Collin's body yet. If it wasn't for your story, no one would know he'd been killed."

"Too late to take back my story?"

"I'm afraid so.

Chapter 14

SIX MONTHS LATER

Eli enters a grove of red maple trees carrying a bamboo pole. He is taller than Noah now and his hair is shoulder-length. Recently, he had taken to wandering away from home, sometimes walking down the road hoping to see Noah, other times frequenting the places they had been together. When he reaches the waterhole they frequented once a week in the summer, he sits on the bank and starts digging with his hand. Six inches into the soil, he finds two juicy worms and fits one on the hook at the end of his nylon fishing line. He tosses the line into the water and waits patiently. He thinks he hears something behind him and looks back into the trees. Nothing. He stares at the water and plants the end of his pole in the wormhole. He starts to doze off, so he lays back and closes his eyes.

Teresa Smith, Rebecca Pearson's swimming hole friend, emerges from the trees with her own bamboo pole. She sits next to Eli, puts a piece of corn on her hook, and casts her line. She removes her black kapp, lets down her long brown hair, and unbuttons the top button of her dress. The fifteen-year-old doesn't have freckles anymore, and she has filled out in all the right places. Eli's pole starts to bend, so she taps him on the shoulder and whispers, "Eli…fish."

Eli wakes up, jumps to his feet, looks around, and says, "Was ist los?" He finally notices he has a fish on the line. "Ich got mei self a fish."

He pulls his line in and proudly displays a small trout. He sits down again, unhooks the fish, and lays it between himself and

Teresa. She frowns, grabs the fish, and throws it back in the water. Eli starts to react, realizes it's a lost cause, and grins.

Teresa raises her chin and chuckles. "Du here for der fish or me?"

Eli scoots over, reaches out, and gently pulls Teresa close to him. "Can ich give du der kiss?"

"Nae, but wir können bundle if du wish."

Teresa grabs her fishing pole and puts it between herself and Eli. They lay back as Eli reaches over and grabs her hand. "Du kommen to mei baptism Sunday?"

"Wo ist das?"

"Right here… im das wasser."

Teresa removes her hand from Eli's hand and whispers "Mei Gott, wir are der sinners to be in das holy place."

Eli takes her hand again. "Nae, wir are datierung."

"Wir are nicht to der dating age yet… sixteen."

"Only zwei months for sie und drei months for mich. Close enough." Eli removes the pole between them and pulls Teresa into his arms. She doesn't resist as they kiss passionately for the first time.

A pestering light rain begins to fall as Eli and Teresa emerge from the trees with their fishing poles propped on their shoulders. Teresa's hair is safely tucked back under her kapp as she follows in Eli's footsteps.

When they reach the road, they look at one another. The air starts to go stale until Eli bites the corner of his lip and revises his smirk into a smile. "Ich will see du at mei baptism."

Teresa tilts her head. "Perhaps." She walks off and Eli heads in the opposite direction. Up ahead, he spots a buggy coming his way. When he realizes it's Malachi Yost and Rebecca Pearson, he stops in his tracks and smiles. Malachi, who is chewing on a carrot, rolls his rig forward and grins. "Eli Hochstetler…it's been a pig's life." Noah's old friend has gained another ten pounds, but Rebecca has lost twenty and is no longer wearing makeup. Malachi looks in the distance as Teresa tops a hill. "Du been playing hide der sausage with Teresa?"

Eli's face turns red. "Huh?... Nae."

Malachi thrusts his hips simulating the sexual act. Rebecca slaps Malachi's arm. "Stoppen, du naughty boy."

Malachi laughs. "Er knows what ich talk about."

Eli tries to explain. "Wir meet here to fish on Thursdays."

"So, where's der fish?"

Eli smiles. "Still in der wasser. Why aren't du driving der truck?"

Malachi grins at Rebecca like he's her lap dog. "Ich gave it up for dis frau. I'm Old Amish again."

Eli studies Rebecca who appears to be besotted by Malachi and asks, "Du a couple?"

Malachi cackles. "Ja, wer about to be married."

Eli squeezes his lips together as he looks at Rebecca. "Du said du was going to marry mei brother."

Rebecca recoils and straightens her kapp. "Das ist long time ago… only because ich saw him nackt."

Malachi leans towards Rebecca. "Du saw Noah naked?"

"Teresa and ich were at der fishing hole and he came out of der wasser before ich could close mei eyes. Now, ich only have eyes for du."

Eli calmly says, "Thought du were cousins?"

Rebecca stiffens. "Second cousins mit der familie blessing."

Malachi changes the subject. "Any wort on der brother?"

"Nae."

"He's der living the life ich always wanted to live… on der sheep."

Eli grins. "Der saying ist on der lamb… And he's not wanted anymore. Die polizei have dropped der charges."

Rebecca slaps Malachi's arm again and says, "On der sheep."

Eli stares at Malachi. "Nicht mehr chewing tobacco?"

Rebecca tilts her chin. "Er gave it up for me. It's a nasty habit."

Eli starts to leave. "Got to go heim. Mei stomach ist growling."

Malachi yells, "Hungry dogs run faster!"

Rebecca elbows Malachi. "Why du say things like das?"

"Ich say I love du."

Rebecca removes a scone from the pocket of her dress, hands it to Malachi, lays her head on his shoulder, and whispers, "And ich liebe dich zu big man."

Malachi flutters his eyes and starts to hum *When the Saints Go Marching In*. He slaps leather to the horse and they roll off. A few seconds later, Malachi says, "Does Noah have a big penis?"

Eli slows to a walk as the rain continues to fall. He tilts his head to the sky and starts to think about Noah and how he hasn't seen his brother for almost two years. The police had been to the farm a few times looking for him, but they never said if they had any idea where he had been or where he was headed. It was hard for Eli to believe his brother had killed someone. He had never even killed a farm animal unless you count the pig he landed on when he jumped out of the barn. There was a part of Eli that wanted to leave home and search for Noah, but he figured if the police couldn't find him what chance would he have?

The rain lets up as Eli nears home, where he sees his father repairing a corner post in the pig pen. In the garden, his mother is harvesting vegetables and pulling weeds.

When Eli enters the front yard, his fishing pole still on his shoulder, Moses turns his way. "Du late kommen for dein chores."

"Sorry, Vader. Ich will do them now."

"Du fisch alone?"

Eli is tempted to lie, but he tells his father the truth. "Ich war mit Rebecca Smith."

"War du familiar mit ihr?"

"Wir kissed, but das war alles."

Moses quotes First Corinthians 6:18-19 in English: "'Flee fornication. Every sin that a man doeth is without the body; be he that committeth fornication sinneth against his own body.'"

Eli bristles. "Es wars only a kiss."

Surprised by Eli's reaction, Moses mutters, "Wir werden spreche about das later."

Moses watches his son leave as Ruth rubs her dirty hands on her apron and walks over to him. She speaks firmly. "I've been dein obedient frau and have been respectful of dein wishes for all diese years, but der way du treat our children needs zu change."

Moses growls, "Du sprechen to mich like das?"

"Ja, ich do.

Moses raises his chin. "Continue dann."

Ruth raises her chin. "Du used der wort of Gott in such a way as to force our oldest sohn to leave unser home… and if du continue Eli will gehen his way as well."

Moses defends himself. "Ich only sprechen Gott's truth."

Ruth doesn't give in. "Gott's truth ist more than der rules and scripture. Es ist love and forgiveness."

He tries again. "Ich war trying to protect Eli from entering into sexual indiskretion."

Ruth touches her husband's arm. "Ich war a month pregnant mit Noah when wir married and told everyone er arrived early? Du resented him because of das. Es war nicht his fault. Forgiveness blesses de giver as well der receiver."

Cold and sparing, Moses backs away and says, "Ich asked Gott for forgiveness."

"But du never asked Noah for forgiveness. Ich am sure Gott has forgiven du and still loves du, but diese familie needs zu know du love them. Du cannot repair a broken cup with regret."

Moses narrows his eyes. "Ich work hard and take care of mei families's needs."

"But our children need zu know du love them. Du have not hugged or kissed or said du loved them for a long time… and du have not touched mich for too many years."

Moses looks away and mutters. "Thought, wir wären finished having children."

"Sex ist nicht just for having der children, but ich would be happy with soft worten, a gentle touch, and a buggy ride by your side."

"Perhaps it is too late for mich zu change."

"If Gott kann love us after wir sin, wir kann love one another again. Ich need zu love du more than ich do now. Du are a stubborn man Moses Hochstetler, but Gott kann soften dein heart, just as er has softened mei heart for du."

Moses removes his hat and walks into the barn while Ruth returns to the garden.

Moses sits on the barn roof with his legs dangling over the edge thinking about how he and his wife were hot and cold working against each other. They had been creating icicles for years now.

A barn owl lands on the weathervane with a dead mouse in its talons. Moses stares at the bird as it pecks at its prey. He grumbles, "Herr Eule!. What makes du think du are so wise? If du know so much, where ist mei oldest sohn? Am ich responsible for driving him away? Ich just wanted him to serve Gott der way ich do, but now mei wife says ich am not capable of showing love. Gott ist it zu late for mich? Will du soften mei heart? Will du help mich love mei familie again?"

Moses closes his eyes and the owl flutters its wings and flies off. When he opens them again, he looks down from the barn roof and sees his family finishing their work in the garden. He takes a moment, listens to them laughing, and yells, "Hello down there!"

Ruth looks up at the barn roof and sees Moses standing on the edge. Her eyes suggest she thinks he's about to jump, so she screams, "Moses Hochstetler, get down from dort before du hurt yourself!"

The children snicker as Moses looks down at Ruth and smiles. "Going to hook up der buggy for our date. Meet du in front of der haus in ten minutes."

The children turn to their mother and giggle as Ruth wipes her hands on her apron and heads for the house.

Minutes later, Moses and Ruth, who is wearing a bright yellow dress, ride off in their buggy as all the Hochstetler children, including Eli, watch. They cheer and wave at their parents as Eli's face suggests he doesn't know what to think.

On a clear sky Sunday afternoon, Eli stands waist-deep in the waterhole next to his father. On the shoreline are several Amish families who are waiting for Eli to get baptized. A few outsiders are in attendance, including Teresa Smith, who is dressed in her Sunday finest.

Moses places his hand on Eli's head and calmly says, "Gott, ich ask das du bless mei son, Eli Hochstetler, who goes into the waters of baptism of his own free will. Cleanse his heart and fill it mit dein Holy Spirit… And give him der joy of knowing his familie loves him."

Eli pinches his nose and his father lowers his son's entire body under the water. When Eli emerges, he wipes his face and smiles, while the witnesses on shore clap softly. He hesitates, hugs his father, and wades to shore. Several women begin to lay out blankets and empty picnic baskets for an afternoon meal.

When Eli steps out of the water, he spots Teresa and walks over to her. He hesitates a moment and wipes his hands on his wet trousers. He offers her his right hand and she shakes it. Teresa dabs her moist hand on her dress, hides it behind her back, and kisses him on the cheek. Eli's mother notices the display of affection, turns, and smiles.

Chapter 15

In snow-covered Banff National Park, two miles south of the municipality itself, Noah checks two wire snares and finds a snowshoe rabbit and a Columbian ground squirrel. Noah, looking like he's been drug through the woods, drops his dinner in a burlap bag and ties it shut with an old shoelace. Then he wipes his blood-stained hands on his already filthy trousers and walks away.

Minutes later, in a small clearing deep in the woods, the homeless man watches the rabbit and squirrel roast over an open fire. His faded quilt covers his shoulders as he puts a frying pan filled with chickweed, dandelion greens, and strawberry spinach in the fire under the smoking meat.

His hair is long, his beard is scraggly, and he has lost twenty pounds. If it wasn't for the stocking cap covering his head and his ill-fitted clothes and mustache, he could easily be mistaken for a married Amish man.

Finished with his meal, Noah looks in his duffel bag for something sweet to eat, but it's empty. Frustrated, he kicks out the fire, gathers his belongings, and walks away.

The sun peeks through an abundance of clouds, Noah trudges through the snow. He stops, looks in the distance, and sees a dozen big horn sheep scaling the side of Mount Rundle. He aims his pistol, realizes the sheep are too far away, and resumes his trek through the forest.

A little further down the trail, he brushes the limb of an evergreen tree and a pile of snow falls off, covering his tattered bus driver coat. He continues until he reaches an open meadow, where he sees four elk grazing. He aims his gun and fires twice. The elk run off as Noah pulls the trigger again... click... nothing... out of bullets.

Back on the snow-packed trail, he spots a log cabin in the distance. Beyond it is a rank of massive pine tree sentinels with the winter sun rising above them, giving the cabin a golden glow. As he nears the building, he notices a curtain-less window and peeks inside. He pushes hard on the back door and to his surprise it opens. Noah shyly checks out the kitchen and the three bedrooms, making sure he has the place all to himself. When he goes back to the kitchen, he opens a few cupboards, where he finds a loaf of bread, cans of vegetables and soup, and jars of peanut butter and jelly. He slides over to the refrigerator and removes a carton of milk and a bowl of red Jello.

Finally, he opens a drawer, grabs a spoon and knife, sits at the kitchen table, and makes himself lunch. As he gobbles down a peanut butter and jelly sandwich, he drinks milk from the carton with one hand and scoops a huge spoonful of Jello in his mouth with the other.

Satisfied, Noah walks to the master bedroom and opens a closet, where he finds a variety of men's clothing. He removes what he is wearing, including his bus coat, and tosses everything on the floor. Like a man shopping in a department store, he removes two flannel shirts, a hooded blue parka, and a pair of jeans from the hangers. Wearing nothing but his skivvies, he holds his new clothes in front of a mirror.

Dressed in his new digs that are too big for him, he waits for a dryer to finish its spin cycle. When it stops, he removes his quilt and wraps it around his neck, enjoying its warmth. He returns to the kitchen, where he stuffs his duffel bag with cans of food, bread, and a variety of condiments. On the counter, he spots a plate of chocolate chip cookies. He carefully places them in his duffel bag and zips it shut. He starts to leave but steps back. He unzips his bag, puts three cookies back on the plate, and walks out of the cabin.

At another campsite, seated on a dead tree in front of a fire, Noah nibbles on a stolen cookie. He licks his fingers, grabs his bag, unzips it, and smiles at the rest of his bounty. Then he moves to his sleeping bag, crawls inside, and puts the quilt on top for extra warmth.

The next morning, Noah stands in front of a mirror in yet another cabin munching on a cookie, while he tries to attach a pair of suspenders to his pants. He finally figures it out and then places a black fedora hat on his head, like the one he wore to Sunday services when he lived in Amish country. Satisfied with his new look, he enters a second bedroom, where he finds several toys, including a Duncan yo-yo. He tries it out but has trouble making it work. Next, he grabs a slinky and stretches it out, unsure how to use it. He puts it back, adjusts his hat and suspenders, and exits the cabin.

Later that afternoon, having been bitten by the thievery bug, Noah waits behind a pine tree as vacation cabin owners, David and Melinda Mahoney, pack up their van, preparing to leave.

Noah looks over at the Mahoney garden. He missed seeing the sprouting vegetables in the garden plot outside his Amish home, the smell of boiling sweet corn in a five-gallon pot, and the taste of homemade butter and raspberry jam on his mother's freshly baked bread.

His brow dampens as he thinks about what he's about to do… rob another cabin. What would his mother think? He remembered when she took some vegetables to sell at the Farmers' Market in Strasburg and someone stole all her wicker baskets. She didn't understand why they took them but forgave them anyway.

He hated the fact that he still cared what his folks thought. As he continued to try to justify the murders and now the thievery, he kept reminding himself that the men he killed deserved to die and that the cabins he had robbed had more crap in them than the owners knew what to do with. Of course, he also realized his family wouldn't see it that way. As he continued to think about them, he wondered why God had picked him to be the son of an Amish deacon. Was everything in life only a matter of chance? What if his father hadn't gotten frisky one night and impregnated his mother? What if he had waited a few days? Would he have turned out to be the same person? Who knows? He might have ended up being his father's pride and joy, a God-fearing farmer, who loved to plow the ground and raise pigs. Right now, everything seemed hopeless. Was he destined to spend the rest of his life searching for food and a place to sleep like the prodigal son? He hadn't slept with any pigs yet, but he hated the way he was living, and he certainly didn't want to keep looking over his shoulder for the authorities.

The Mahoney's start their vehicle and drive off, so Noah walks to the back of the cabin and tries to open the door. It won't budge, so he breaks a glass panel, reaches inside, and unlocks the door.

Noah is seated at a small kitchen table eating a grapefruit he found in the refrigerator. He lays his spoon down, stands up, goes to the stove, and salts the scrambled eggs still cooking in a cast iron skillet. While he waits for his breakfast, he goes to the counter, finds a cookie jar, and fits a handful in the pocket of his new parka.

Suddenly he hears a vehicle approaching. He looks out the window and watches as the Mahoney van returns and David Mahoney parks under a carport near the back door. He panics and rushes to the front of the house. He finds a door, struggles with the lock, shoves the door open, and runs off.

As Melinda Mahoney gets out of the van she turns to her husband and grumbles, "Sorry, David, but I need my knitting bag. It's a long way home."

When they reach the back door, David freezes. "What do we have here? Broken glass all over the place, eh." The couple sidesteps the shards and cautiously enters the kitchen, where they are greeted by the smell of burning eggs.

Melinda hurries to the gas stove and turns off the burner. She scans the living room. "Oh my God! Someone's in our cabin."

"I left my gun at home. We should leave, eh."

"Yeah, no. We… you need to protect what's ours." Melinda grabs a fire extinguisher from under the sink and hands it to her husband. "Here, use this."

With Melinda carrying a cast iron pot behind him, David leads the way as the couple searches their cabin one room at a time. When they return to the living room, David notices the front door is slightly ajar. "Look, he must have heard us coming and escaped out the front door."

Satisfied the place is empty, they return to the kitchen, where after a closer inspection they find a dinner plate, a glass of milk, and two slices of toast. Melinda looks the room over again and sees a brown paper bag sitting on a kitchen chair. She peeks inside it and removes three cans of soup and two boxes of crackers. "Lucy Carmichael said there have been a lot of cabin break-ins lately. Someone stealing food and clothes, and helping themselves to anything they want, especially cookies.

Melinda walks over to her kitchen counter, removes the lid from the cookie jar, and looks inside. She holds the empty jar out to David, who rolls his eyes and says, "The Cookie Bandit strikes again."

It's early evening in the Banff City Hall. The town mayor, sixty-year-old Charles Knox, is seated between two town council members, Edith Smith, and Ted Burnside. Across from them are twenty community members, including David and Melinda Mahoney, who are talking to the people around them.

The mayor raps his gavel on the table, and everyone quiets down. "So, let's get right to it, eh. I called you here tonight because we have a thief in the area who has been breaking into cabins." He points at the Mahoney's and says, "David and Melinda Mahoney here almost caught him in the act, but what some of you are calling the Cookie Bandit managed to get away."

A local insurance salesman in the back of the room cups his hands and yells, "Why Cookie Bandit?"

David turns to the man and addresses the question. "He steals all sorts of things, but always cookies."

People laugh and the mayor continues. "Other than cookies, what else did he take?"

David stands up. "Nothing we know of. When we returned to the cabin, we must have scared him off. He was in the middle of making himself some scrambled eggs. Found a bag of food and other things on the table he was about to take with him." Melinda whispers in her husband's ear and he addresses the crowd. "They were homemade molasses cookies."

People laugh as a silver-haired woman taps David on the shoulder and whispers, "Took my late husband's favorite wool socks and some cookies too… at least a dozen."

An insurance salesman yells, "Missing my blue parka, a pair of pants, and two flannel shirts. Left me a dirty bus driver coat on a hanger like it was a fair trade. Coat had a name on it and the name of a bus company on the back."

The mayor sits up straight. "Well, what was it?"

"The nametag was tattered, but it looked to be Kyle. Bus company I can't remember… Canadian something or other."

"Well, bring it to my office when you get a chance. It's evidence."

"Can't do that. I burned it. It smelled real bad."

People laugh again and talk as a middle-aged woman with a ponytail shouts, "Stole my son's birthday cake before he even got a piece… and a ham!"

Mildred Jensen, a local nurse, says, "I don't mind him taking a few things if he's hungry."

The town's lone barber, Ned Bruce, leans over and says, "That's like feeding a grizzly bear, Mildred. We don't want him making a habit of busting in our homes and helping himself."

People chatter away as Lester Jefferies, a local restaurant owner, speaks his mind. "I'm missing a sledgehammer, a tree saw, and my favorite fishing pole. It was a real beaut."

Ned grins. "I borrowed your pole, Lester. I'll give it back to you tomorrow."

People laugh as Lester glares at Ned. "Still, my hammer and saw, eh."

Local hairdresser, Francis Miller pipes up. "Cleaned out my fridge and cupboards and I'm missing two dozen store-bought chocolate chip cookies."

People talk even louder, so the mayor holds up his hand. "Okay, settle down. Appears this so-called Cookie Bandit has a sweet tooth. Secure your cabins when you leave and lock your doors for God's sake. Other than the Mahoney's here, everyone I've talked to admitted their doors weren't even locked."

Middle-aged outdoorsman and bird watcher, Baxter Carson, raises his hand, and the mayor nods. "What is it, Baxter?"

"Might have a picture of the bugger," Baxter holds up an enlarged black-and-white photo and people gather around him to get a good look. The photograph reveals Noah's backside as he sits in front of a fire with his mother's quilt wrapped around him.

Lester peeks over the photographer's shoulder and studies the photo. "That's my sledgehammer… right there next to him."

The insurance salesman says, "And he's wearing my parka."

The mayor holds out his hand. "Let me see that, Baxter." The bird watcher gives Charles the photo as the other council members, Edith and Ted, join the mayor and study the photograph.

Edith lowers her glasses. "Can't see his face."

Ted laughs. "Could be the Sasquatch or Bigfoot for all we know."

The mayor says, "Well, at least this is a start."

Ted shakes his head. "There's no telling who that is."

Lester shouts. "Telling you that's my sledgehammer!"

The insurance salesman adds, "And my coat."

The mayor looks at Baxter and says, "Why'd you take this picture, Baxter?"

I don't know. I was bird-watching east of town and there he was. Sometimes I take photos of unusual things. I didn't want to interrupt the guy, so I snapped his picture and kept moving."

Edith speaks up. "Kind of creepy, Baxter. He's not a bird."

Charles hands the man back his photo and addresses the room. "Okay, like I said, keep your doors locked and eat your damn cookies before the cookie monster gets them."

Edith whispers loud enough to be heard. "Cookie Bandit!"

Everyone laughs except for Melinda and David Mahoney. Melinda stares at the mayor and pouts, "I don't think you should make light of this, mayor. We don't know what he is capable of."

People leave as the mayor looks at Melinda and says, "You're right. You're right. Everyone be safe."

As people filter out of the room, Roxy Durrant, a local news reporter, walks over to Baxter and says, "May I borrow that photo, Baxter? I'd like to write a story about our local Cookie Bandit."

Baxter hands her the photo and smiles. "Be my guest."

Two days later in Niagara Falls, Ontario, Morgan Winston is lying on his couch drinking a beer and eating salt and vinegar potato chips from a bag resting on his chest. The hockey game he's watching ends, so he gets up and switches the channel to the national news that's just wrapping up.

He heads back to his couch as broadcaster, Marcus Sorenson, finishes a story. The middle-aged anchor, wearing a tan suit and a blue silk tie, looks over at Terri Glenn, a pretty weatherwoman in a blue dress. The camera focuses on her face and then pans back to Marcus.

The newsman points at the camera. "Finally, tonight, a story out of Banff National Park and the town of Banff itself. A man in the area has been breaking into cabins and stealing an assortment of things. However, it appears the alleged thief has a fondness for cookies. Residents report that the thief has stolen clothes, tools, and food, but always steals cookies. Here's a photo of the man the locals are calling The Cookie Bandit."

The black and white photo Baxter took appears on the screen. Morgan sits up and looks at his TV closely. When he sees a quilt draped around the man's shoulders and a duffel bag at his feet, he narrows his eyes.

Terri laughs. "So, Marcus, does that mean the citizens of Banff are on the lookout for a thief with crumbs on his face?"

"Very clever, Terri, but don't give up your day job. Unfortunately for the people of Banff, no one has seen his face. He does however have a nice-looking quilt."

As the snow falls, Morgan Winston drives down Main Street Banff. He parks his car, spots a mailman, and asks for directions. The letter carrier points and Morgan jaywalks across the street. He enters the Knox Insurance Agency and asks to see Charles Knox.

In the mayor's office, Morgan waits while Charles looks Noah Hochstetler's wanted poster over. He curls his lip. "So, what makes you think this is our thief? No one's seen his face."

"Might be a waste of time, but in that photo, there was a quilt around the suspect's shoulders and a duffel bag at his feet. The man I'm looking for had both those items."

The mayor hands the poster back to Morgan. "Didn't know we were dealing with a killer. This isn't good."

"This is an old poster and the murders are turning out to be justifiable homicides. Still, I need to find him."

"Noah? Sure his name isn't Kyle?"

"Did you find his coat?"

"I didn't, but somebody else did. Said it had the name of some Canadian bus company on the back."

"I'd like to see it?"

"You can't. The idiot burned it."

"Doesn't matter. He's our man."

"Okay, how can I help?"

"I want to form a search party and see if I can find him."

"Constable, do you know how big our park is? He could be anywhere."

"Has he broken into any other cabins lately?"

"Yes, mine... two days ago. But don't tell anyone. I'm up for election in a month."

Morgan tries not to smile. "You missing any cookies?"

"Brownies and a box of matches."

Chapter 16

Sergeant Winston stands tall on the outskirts of Banff in a parking lot surrounded by pine trees with five men: Mayor Charles Knox, Baxter Carson, David Mahoney, and two male park rangers in their mid-twenties.

Nearby are Melinda Mahoney, Roxy Durrant, and two thirty-plus-year-old local female hikers from Banff. The sergeant steps forward, squares his chest, and says, "Okay, the last known break-in was at the mayor's place on Thursday." He turns to Charles and whispers, "Sorry." Then he addresses the rest of the search party. "Our fugitive is more than likely still in the area. I don't think he's dangerous, but I don't know that for sure. He may or may not have a weapon. We'll fan out in groups of three. I'm giving each group leader a whistle. If you see anyone or anything suspicious, blow it and stay where you are. Do not approach the man and try to apprehend him. That's my job. Everyone hear what I said?"

The posse volunteers nod and Winston hands the mayor and Baxter each a whistle. He keeps one and signals the male park rangers to join him.

The next group, made up of Baxter, David, Melinda, and Roxy heads north, while the mayor and the female hikers start south. Sergeant Winston waves the young rangers to follow him and they head west.

Morgan and his two men trudge down a snow-covered path dodging branches and hopping over deadfall trees. The sergeant spots a clearing and holds up his hand. He considers his options and waves the men to follow him down a steep bank. Slipping and sliding, they reach the bottom of the hill and discover a small smoldering fire pit. As Morgan looks for other signs of life, he spots fresh tracks leading away from the campsite. "Stay right here. I'm going to follow these tracks."

One of the rangers says, "I thought we were supposed to stick together."

"Stay here in case he comes back. I have a weapon and you don't. I'm going to try to catch up with him. I don't want anyone getting shot at unless it's me. Hear a whistle or gunfire, follow my tracks 'til you find me." The sergeant walks off and the young rangers, look at one another, shrug their shoulders, and plop down on a dead tree.

Following the tracks, Sergeant Winston struggles up a snow-covered ridge. At the top, he looks for more footprints but doesn't see any. He finds a path and walks ahead until it dead ends at a cliff overlooking the Bow River. He takes a few steps, edging closer. He looks at the rushing water, hears someone behind him, and swings around. He realizes who it is, so he reaches for his revolver, but it's too late. Standing six feet away, Noah points his gun directly at Morgan. In his left hand, he is clutching his quilt and duffel bag. There's a moment of awkward silence and then the runaway calmly says, "Don't make me shoot you."

The sergeant lifts his chin. "Noah… Hochstetler."

"I knew you would find me. What took so long?"

"I know your story and I'm sure this past year has been hell. But Sally Ann told us her father tried to drop an anvil on you and you were only trying to defend yourself."

"I'm guessing Chad Livingston told you I killed his professor?"

"He did say that at first. But then on the way home, he admitted he was the one who shot Professor Collins to keep him from stabbing you. After we got back to Toronto, he changed his story again and said Collins wasn't dead at all. He simply went crazy and ran off. With no dead body or evidence, the police had to let him go. Now Livingston and Collins are nowhere to be found. Truth is Noah, you don't have to run anymore."

"I killed Sergeant Hanson."

"I know, but investigators found out Hanson had a history of sexually abusing recruits. Two soldiers came forward after they heard what happened and told authorities he forced himself on them while they were in boot camp.

"But I butchered him like a pig." Noah tightens his grip on his gun and raises it.

Morgan steps back, expecting the worst. "You don't want to do that, son."

Noah knew there were no bullets in the gun, but the policeman didn't know it. Why was the officer being nice, like he cared about him? Was he just trying to calm him down, so he could arrest him and collect some reward?

Noah runs past Morgan and free falls a hundred feet into the Bow River, hits the water hard, and disappears below the surface. The sergeant looks down from the cliff but doesn't see Noah emerge from the water. What he does see is the young man's red duffel bag and multi-colored quilt float to the top, start down the river, and disappear around a curve. The sergeant walks over, picks up Noah's gun, and tries to fire a warning shot. Click. He wags his head, sits on a nearby boulder, and blows his whistle.

The next morning below the cliff seated in a ten-passenger rescue boat filled with diving equipment, Morgan and Baxter look for signs of life in the Bow River. As the small outboard motor purrs, two scuba divers emerge from the water and swim over to the side of the craft. One of the divers looks at Morgan and says,

"Nothing. Current most likely carried him downstream for miles. Might not find him until spring… if at all. Did find the blanket you told us about, but no bag." The divers struggle as they shove the water-soaked quilt up into the boat.

Morgan climbs back in the boat near the shoreline as Baxter and the divers give him curious looks. Baxter breaks the silence. "Why'd you do that?

Slow to answer, Morgan says, "If he did drown, I can't think of a better grave marker." As the boat motors away, a large rock with Noah's quilt draped over it is revealed.

A Pennsylvania state police car drives up and parks in front of Moses Hochstetler's farmhouse. Two officers walk slowly to the front door, remove their hats, and knock. Moses, whose beard is turning grey, opens the door. He's wearing his black hat. The senior officer straightens his shoulders and says, "Got some bad news for you, sir. We think your son drowned in the Bow River in Banff National Park last week. Recovery team didn't find his body but they're pretty sure he didn't survive the icy water."

Moses speaks English. "Do you think he took his own life?"

The senior policeman replies, "According to the investigating officer, that is a possibility. Jumping in the river was his choice." Moses doesn't say anything, so the man continues, "As you know, your son was wanted for murder, but he has been cleared of all charges, including breaking into cabins in Banff National Park in Alberta, Canada. The people there aren't pressing charges."

The younger officer hands the Amish farmer a business card. "If for some reason you see him, give us a call. We'd still like to talk to him." Moses looks at the card briefly and closes the door.

Chapter 17

Two Weeks Later

It's an early spring morning as Ruth Hochstetler leaves the house with a rolled-up carpet and walks to the clothesline. She drops the rug when she sees Noah's quilt hanging on the line. She looks in the distance and spots a young man walking down the road away from the farm at a brisk pace. "Noah! Noah! Ist das du?" The stranger doesn't look back, so she lowers her head and removes the quilt from the clothesline. She smells it, drapes it around her shoulders, and hurries into the house.

Eli enters the house and walks into the living room, where he finds his father consoling his mother, who is bent over Noah's quilt and crying. He sides up to her and says, "Vas is los, Mutter?"

She doesn't answer, so Eli glares at his father who says, "Du go find dein bruder und bring ihn heim."

"Wo do I look?"

"Dein mutter säge ihn gehen east an der foot."

Eli hurries out of the house and straight for the barn. He quickly attaches the traces to the buggy and the breast collar to the horse's neck. Then he crawls up into the seat and clucks the reins.

As he steers the buggy down the road, he looks right and left as he searches for his brother. Had Noah returned home just to leave a quilt for his mother to find? Why hadn't he at least taken the time to greet his family, especially his favorite brother?

A mile down the road, Eli's thoughts turn to anger and he screams, "Noah! Don't leave! We need to talk!" He pulls up on the reins, the horse stops, and he looks out into the open fields. With harvest season over, the dark soil is devoid of any vegetation. Eli starts to turn the buggy around for home when in the distance he sees what appears to be his brother in the middle of the road walking his way.

Eli slaps leather to the horse and the buggy lurches forward. When the animal reaches the unfamiliar man, he comes to a stop on his own. Noah's clothes are tattered and filthy and he is holding his faded red duffel bag. His face is gaunt and he has a scraggly beard that hasn't been trimmed in months. He's wearing a faded red ball cap that covers his long dirty hair and his fingernails are long and clouded with dirt. The brothers stare at one another until Eli speaks, "Du look like a schwein in der muck."

After years of immersion in the outside world, Noah speaks perfect English with a hint of Pennsylvania Dutch. "Danke. Du look pretty good yourself."

"Where du gehen? Vader wishes du to be heim."

"Not my home anymore."

"Heim ist familie."

"I'm on the run from the law. I'm wanted for murder."

"Der police told Vader all charges against du have ended."

"Don't lie to me."

"Vader does not lie. I do not lie. Du kommst nach hause."

"I am a filthy vagabond."

"Mutter will waschen der kleidung."

Noah changes the subject. "You are much bigger than me now."

"Und stronger zu."

Noah grins as he studies Eli's profile. "Du look like him. Is he working you to death?"

"Nae, ich am attending school in Strasburg. Ich want to learn more so I can own mei own business and sell der furniture."

Noah chuckles. "Did a horse kick him in the head?"

"Noah, Vader ist wicher… softer now."

"If you say so. I would like to see Mutter and mei brothers and sisters. Have they grown like weeds?"

"Ja, all of them."

"Du have a schnuckiputzi?"

"Ja, Teresa Smith."

"The little girl from the waterhole?"

"Ja, not so wenig anymore… but she's seen du naked and nicht me."

"For your sake, I hope that changes."

Eli reaches into his pocket and removes the unicorn Noah whittled for him before he left home. "Remember das?"

He takes it from Eli, looks it over, and breaks off the unicorn's horn.

Eli grabs it back and accesses the damage. "Warum tun das?"

"I gave that to you that thinking I was like that unicorn… one of a kind. But I'm like everyone else."

"Nae, you're not. You're mei bruder." Eli takes the reins. "Kommen, wir gohen heim."

Noah hesitates and climbs into the buggy next to his brother. Eli yells, "Gohen, Bessy!" The horse trots away headed for home. As they ride along, Noah looks at Eli and says, "You a God-fearing man like Vader now?"

"Ich got baptized."

"That's not what I asked."

Eli takes a deep breath. "Ich believe that even if there is no Gott, dreaming there ist one makes mei world a lot better."

Noah smiles. I like that. I like that a lot."

When the boys arrive home, the front door opens and Noah's siblings run out and surround the buggy. They take turns hugging Noah as his mother and father watch from the front porch. Ten-year-old Anna, the last to hug him, grabs her nose and grimaces. "Du schtinke." He laughs and smells his shirt. Then he studies his brothers and sisters, who have grown considerably in the last two and a half years.

His mother can't wait any longer and hurries down the steps to hug him. After a long embrace, she says, "Willkommen heim, mei lost sohn."

She turns back to Moses and nods. He raises his chin and walks down the steps to his oldest son. When he reaches Noah, he stares at him and smiles. "Sie sind gewachsen into a fine-looking mann." He looks into Noah's eyes and continues in broken English. "Ich ask for dein forgiveness for being so stiff-necked and being der asshole."

Noah steps back, unsure how to respond. Finally, he offers his hand for his father to shake. Moses grabs it and pulls Noah into his arms. As they hug, Moses begins to cry. He whispers in Noah's ear. "Du be whatever it ist du wish to be and gehen anywhere du wish to gehen as long as du kommen heim for den visit."

The family gathers around Noah again as they enter the house. Ruth scoots over to her son and holds out her hand. He takes the hint, removes his shirt, and hands it to her. He starts to unbuckle his pants, but she waves him off.

Noah is submerged underwater in the family bathtub. Suddenly, he sits up and takes a deep breath. His thoughts turn to his family and the peace he felt being home. Eli was right. His father had softened. He hadn't even mentioned God or quoted scripture at him. The truth was Noah had mellowed himself. The anger and resentment he felt for his father, began to melt away as soon as he hugged him. Even before that, after he nearly drowned in the cold water of the Bow River, something changed and he wanted to go home.

When he found his mother's quilt drying on the rock, he immediately thought about his family and the peacefulness of the Amish community where he grew up. Maybe Eli was right. There can be a variety of stages of belief in life, including that there is a God who not only created the world but loves the people he put on the earth to inhabit it. A person doesn't have to be a deacon to appreciate that. As for settling down, marrying an Amish woman, and farming like his father, he figured that probably wouldn't ever happen.

He knew he might have to leave again, but first things first. Noah grabs a bar of homemade soap and scrubs his arms vigorously visualizing the home-cooked meal his mother is already preparing in the kitchen.

As the sun sets, Eli and clean-shaven and well-groomed Noah climb the ladder to the top of the barn. The brothers move to the edge of the roof and look down. They take a moment, grin, and leap off the barn, flapping their arms and screaming, "Geronimo!" They land feet first in the pig pen, sit in the straw, and stare at the sky.

Noah and Eli are about to stand up when their father yells, "Geronimo!" Moses drops from the barn roof as his sons crawl out of his way. When he lands awkwardly on his feet next to them, his hat falls off, revealing his grey and thinning hair. He sits in a pile of straw beside them, rubs his knees, and smiles as Noah and Eli look at one another in disbelief.

The Hochstetler men laugh as the barn owl Moses spoke to earlier circles above them. The bird surveys the farm below, flaps its wings, and flies away.

EPILOGUE

A city bus stops at a University of Toronto kiosk, and Chad Livingston steps out. His hair is cropped short now and his face is freshly shaven. Dressed in tan khaki pants and a white shirt that is neatly pressed, he fits right in with the other students who walk past.

As he surveys the campus looking for changes, he heads toward St. Michael's College, the home for the humanities and theology education programs.

When Chad enters the building, he starts to look for familiar faces... students he might know, professors, even custodians. Finally, Associate Professor Clyde Barron approaches and Chad smiles. "Professor Barron?"

"Chad... Chad Livingston?"

"Yes, sir."

"You're back. Where have you been?"

"Here and there. I needed to take some time off."

"Are you going to finish your thesis? The clock is ticking."

"About that, I might need to start over. Would you be willing to be my advisor?"

"You're Professor Collin's advisee. I don't think he would like that. Ever since he got back, he's been asking about you."

"Kenneth Collins? He's not dead."

Professor Barron chuckles. "Police came around thinking he was dead too. I just saw him a few minutes ago. You've been gone awhile. The book you helped him with is about to be published. He's in the lecture hall right now promoting it."

"And he's all right?"

"Yes, he had a rough spell after the two of you parted ways, but he's doing well, considering what he went through."

"So, after we parted ways… what did he go through?"

"I don't know what happened to you, but they found him wandering in some forest in Manitoba. People in the area claim he was living off the land for six months rambling on about being a Son of David. When the police picked him up, he had a gash on the side of his head that had almost healed, so the doctors thought he might have taken a bad fall… or maybe just had a mental breakdown or a stroke. Collins says he doesn't remember much. His short-term memory was gone for a while and he talked a little slow, but he's recovered well… well enough to go back to teaching. I read his book and it's quite good. I don't know how much of it is true, but you two had some wild adventures. Spoiler alert. In the last chapter, you try to kill him and run off with some crazy-ass woman who thinks the world is about to end." Professor Barron grins. "You didn't do that did you?"

"There was no crazy-ass woman… not on our trip anyway."

"Like the saying goes, life is sometimes stranger than fiction. Lucky for him he had his journals when he got off the train. Once he recovered, he was able to piece together a damn good novel."

"Lecture hall, you say?"

"Right. Good to have you back."

Noah walks down the hallway past Kenneth Collin's office. He checks to see if his advisor's nameplate is still on the door. Still confused, he starts for the lecture hall. When he gets there, he pauses briefly and slips inside. He spots a seat in the back row, passes by a few bored students, and sits down.

When he looks up, he sees Professor Collins. Next to him, leaning against his podium is a wooden cane. As he halfway listens to his old traveling partner's monotone and jerky delivery, he wonders how the man could still be alive. Will Collins remember that he shot him? And even if he doesn't remember now, will seeing him again trigger his memory? He finally focuses on what his old professor is reading and leans forward.

Collins pauses and clears his throat. "'The self-appointed man of God continued to ride the rails searching for disciples who would devote themselves to his new religion. He wanted them to be willing to die for a set of principles he hadn't even thought of yet. Would they be willing to rob a bank, burn down a government building, or even kill a public official? That was the kind of mind-control Sol wanted to have.'"

Suddenly, Professor Collins lays his book aside, looks out at his audience, and asks, "Put in the same predicament as many of the homeless people that Solomon encountered in my novel, how many of you would entertain the idea of joining a new religion made up of like-minded and desperate people?"

A young man in the front row raises his hand and Collins nods. "You mean like joining a cult or following a Charles Manson prototype?"

"Yes. What would you believe or do to survive in an evil world that cares nothing about you? Would you be willing to become another person and bury your old identity? I am talking about a genuine change in personality that everyone around you would accept as the new you."

The young man answers again. "I think your mind-controller character, Solomon is a phony. At least most cult leaders believe their own shit. The only reason Sol changed his identity was so he could feed his ego, manipulate people, and write a book."

"You might be right. My time is up. That concludes my presentation."

As students prepare to leave, Professor Collins looks up at the back row where Chad is still seated. He nods and says, "Son of David, you are home."

Author's Note

The inciting incident that precipitated this novella comes from the exploits of a vagabond named Joseph Henry Burgess, whom local New Mexicans called "The Cookie Bandit."

Burgess left his home in New Jersey in the early 1970s to avoid being drafted into the Vietnam War. He moved to Canada, where he became a "Jesus freak" and a member of the religious cult "Children of God." For a time, he called himself Job Weeks or just Job, having taken his name from the long-suffering Old Testament man of God. The self-proclaimed "prophet of God" made his way across Canada and ended up in Tofino, British Columbia, a small district on Vancouver Island.

Witnesses reported seeing Burgess cleaning his semi-automatic 22-caliber rifle on the beach as he ranted to anyone who would listen about man's sinful nature and the sexual impropriety taking place amongst the masses. Not long after that, he was said to have killed a young unmarried couple who was sleeping together at a campsite near the beach. The theory at the time was Burgess believed the young couple was living in sin and that God wanted them dead.

The Royal Canadian Mounted Police pursued the case, but Joseph Burgess was nowhere to be found. They did find his prescription glasses, a Bible, a shaving kit, boots, and a gun cleaning kit.

Thirty years later in 2004, in an eerily similar case in Northern California, the bodies of another young unwed couple were found dead in their sleeping bags. Authorities believed they had been shot to death while making love. Whether or not Joseph Burgess was responsible for their deaths, has yet to be proven.

In 2005, in the Jemez Mountains fifty-five miles Northwest of Albuquerque, New Mexico, Joseph Burgess surfaced again not far from La Cueva, which sits at over 7,000 feet. The small community is home to both full and part-time cabin dwellers.

Between 2005 and 2011, Joseph was caught on surveillance cameras breaking into cabins in the La Cueva area. Locals reported that he stole among other things, clothes, tools, liquor, and food… but he was especially fond of cookies. The odd thing was that sometimes he left his old garments behind after taking a new set of clothes.

Dubbed the "Cookie Bandit," several people believed he was dangerous and that it was only a matter of time until he injured or killed someone in the area. Some locals claimed to have seen him sitting in front of mysterious campfires, while others said they arrived home shortly after he vacated their cabins.

Authorities set up a stakeout in a local cabin, where two policemen waited for him inside. When he finally took the bait, he crawled through a window where the officers were waiting. One of them wrestled the "Cookie Bandit" to the floor and managed to subdue Burgess. Despite being handcuffed, the bandit was able to shoot the policeman in the leg. A gunfight broke out and Henry Burgess was killed. The second officer was not harmed, but the wounded policeman died at the scene before he could be airlifted back to Albuquerque.

Noah Hochstetler is certainly no Joseph Burgess, but the religious element of Burgess's life, his travels across Canada, and his reputation as the "Cookie Bandit" struck a chord with me. After considering whether to write the true story of the New Mexican "Cookie Bandit," I chose instead to create a fictional tale about a rebellious Amish boy who struggles to find his place in a world that turns out to be very different from his Amish home in rural Pennsylvania.

* As a side note, my wife Martha and I were introduced to the Cookie Bandit story ten years ago when we bought a log cabin in the Jemez Mountains, less than a mile from the cabin where the shootout took place.

ABOUT THE AUTHOR

Daniel Landes retired from South Dakota State University in 2011, where he served as an Assistant Dean of Arts and Sciences and as a professor of English.

Originally from Williston, North Dakota, Dan grew up in Great Falls, Montana, where he graduated from C.M. Russell High School. He went on to earn a Bachelor of Science degree in History at Minot State University, a Master of Science degree in English at Bemidji State University, and a Ph.D. in English from the University of North Dakota. He and his wife Martha live in Rio Rancho, New Mexico, where Dan continues to pursue his love of writing, film production, bicycling, and distance running.

www.ingramcontent.com/pod-product-compliance
Lightning Source LLC
Chambersburg PA
CBHW021714190726
48289CB00008B/2531